# CORA

## ANGEL CREEK CHRISTMAS BRIDES #23

## SYLVIA MCDANIEL

SM

## Twin Mail-Order Brides Running From the Law

After Cora Weaver kills her twin sister's attacker, they flee the law by Cora becoming a mail-order bride. Answering an ad in the *Mail Order Bride Gazette*, the sisters find themselves in the wilds of Angel Creek, Montana. Will the Charleston authorities find them here?

Mack Lawson lost a bet to his brother and now he has to order a mail-order bride. Only Mack isn't certain his wounded heart can accept another cheating woman. When he sees how beautiful Cora is, he knows there's no way she'll be happy in a nowhere place like Angel Creek. With a failed marriage behind him, how can he give his heart a second time?

With Christmas coming, will there be a double wedding or will their pasts tear the couples apart and send Cora to hang? Come back to Angel Creek, Montana, where the Christmas Spirit abounds and a happily ever after is guaranteed.

# CHAPTER 1

Trying to control his frustration, Mack Lawson stared at his younger brother. James knew how he felt about women and yet the man had pushed this stupid bet on him. There wasn't a hot day in January chance of it succeeding.

Standing in the barn of their ranch, right outside of Angel Creek, Montana, a beautiful area filled with pine trees and open spaces, the closest neighbor was miles away. Not a place you lived if you wanted a social life. Not a place you lived unless you liked seclusion.

And most women needed neighbors, friends, and get-togethers. Not here.

Angel Creek was hours from civilization, and in the wintertime, that seemed more like a week.

The baby cows bleated more than mooed, their voices not yet strong. Gazing around the barn, he couldn't believe the number of calves. Every stall was filled with a mother cow and her newborn. Every stinking one of them heifers had managed to have a baby, and while he should be rejoicing because of the bet with his brother, he wasn't.

More babies meant a bigger herd, which meant more money. But right now, he just didn't want to put an ad in a newspaper for a bride.

"A man's word is his honor. You promised me and I succeeded, now it's time for you to do what you said you'd do."

"How the hell did you pull this off? I knew we were going to have a bevy of calves, but I never dreamed we'd have almost fifty. I was expecting more like twenty-five."

James grinned that saucy bewitching smile of his that all the ladies loved. "The bulls were rather randy this year. Do you need any help in placing your ad?"

"No," Mack said with a loud bark. He should never have agreed to do this. It was just one more stupid thing he let his brother convince him to do. The first had been marrying Margery. A sweet, innocent woman at the age of seventeen, who didn't have a clue as to what she wanted in life and soon realized living on a ranch was not her top choice.

"And you're certain all these cows are ours?"

"Yes," his brother said. "Quit stalling. You agreed to this bet. The bulls and I succeeded. Now it's your turn."

Mack glanced around at the barn stalls that had baby cows and the outside fenced area that had older calves.

That bull must have mated with every one of their heifers.

"I never thought we would have more than twenty-five calves born this year. And you know how I feel about marriage."

Mack so wanted to get out of doing this, but knew that if he backed out, his brother would give him hell the rest of his natural life.

His brother nodded. "Time to get over it."

James didn't understand. How did you get over loving a woman who ran off—with a damn pot-and-pan peddler—to what she thought would be a better life that didn't include you?

"Three years have passed since she ran off and then died, and you're still stuck in the past. Move on, Mack."

The most baby calves birthed to their ranch in one year had been twenty-eight. And this year, the winter had been especially rough, so he'd bet no more than thirty. Thinking they would probably come in around twenty-seven. But no! Somehow their cattle had a banner year and produced more baby cows than he'd ever thought possible.

"Which newspaper do you want me to put this advertisement in," Mack asked, thinking he would slide it into something no one would ever see.

"*Mail Order Bride Gazette*," James said. "The biggest newspaper in the country for mail order brides."

Dang my melt! How did he hide an ad in a paper like that?

With a sigh, Mack shook his head. "You're really going to make me do this. Even though you know how I don't need a woman. Especially after everything I've been through."

His brother nodded. "Put the past behind you and move on. If we're going to make this ranch successful, we need women by our sides. A wife and mother of our children and I don't want it to just be me."

For over a year now, James had been harping on this very subject. It was time to help his little brother find his own bride. Without Mack.

He could do this. He would follow James's instructions, but he would put his own special twist on it.

"All right, I'll put together the ad, and the next time I'm in town, I'll put it in the *Mail Order Bride Gazette*."

James shook his head. "Not good enough. It's spring. You and I both know the pass closes the first of November. That gives you six months to correspond with the girl and convince her to move to the deep woods of Montana."

He shrugged. "I can't produce a miracle."

"No, but we need some supplies in town. We'll go in together tomorrow and put your ad in the gazette. It will take at least a month just to get it listed in the newspaper."

He smiled at his brother, knowing already what he wanted to say. "On one condition. I get to write up the ad however I please."

"I think I should get final approval."

4

"Nope. It's my ad. My wishes and I'll put it in there anyway I damn well please. Or the deal's off."

He shrugged. "All right, but remember your word is your honor."

"Yeah, I know," he said, regretting that he was an honest man.

After James walked out of the ranch office, Mack smiled. Oh yes, he would create an ad that any woman who answered it would be a fool to accept. By the time they read his ad, they would be running in the opposite direction.

James may have won the bet, but Mack would win by remaining single.

ora Weaver knew things had to change. She and her sister were stuck in Charleston, North Carolina. Though they had money, there were no men who wanted to court and eventually marry the crazy Weaver twins.

Their parents had not exactly been known as fine upstanding citizens. Her mother hid in her room and her father was a drunk. And yet they managed to somehow hang onto their cash during the Civil War, which could not be said for most of the people in Charleston.

That cash put a target on the girls' backs. Marry a crazy Weaver girl and be set for life or so some believed. And the suitors came and went like the flowing of the tide. None had been acceptable. All courting ended in disaster.

At least for Cora, because she refused to let a man

take advantage of her or court her just for her money. Charleston was loaded with Scalawags, Union soldiers, and men who were trying to rebuild their fortunes. She wasn't there to help.

Not one made her heart flutter and her insides tighten. All of them reminded her of her father and not in a good way.

She sat in her bedroom reading the *Mail Order Bride Gazette*. It was a newspaper she'd picked up on a whim, just to see what it was about. With a toss of her dark hair, she gazed about the room.

What would it be like to choose a husband from a newspaper? To wed a man she'd never seen. At least he would not have any preconceived ideas about the Weaver twins, as they were known.

She stumbled across an ad and laughed. The man at least had a sense of humor and he lived a long ways away. Montana. They weren't even part of the Union.

A loud noise came from the parlor.

Was that a lamp breaking? Was Beth, her twin, in trouble? Harrison Dane had been courting Beth. The man was the son of a prominent congressman, and frankly, Cora felt uneasy around him. There was something about him she didn't like and she wasn't quite sure what it was.

The man was poised and polished, handsome as sin, but when he looked at her sister, she wanted to protect her from him. The man seemed to gaze at her like he wanted to strip her naked. And that frightened Cora.

A scream came from the parlor and Cora jumped up and hurried down the stairs. She lifted her skirts and ran to help her sister. When she entered the room, the man had her on the settee, his body covering hers, his hand beneath her skirts.

"Stop, Harrison. Stop right now," Beth told him.

"Get off my sister," she screamed at him. The man ignored her and continued trying to pull Beth's bloomers down.

Cora ran to the fireplace, picked up the wood poker, and with all her strength, hit him on his back. It didn't faze him. Finally, she lifted the poker and hit him on the back of his head. A big gash appeared and he slumped on top of Beth.

She shoved him with all her might. "Get him off me. He was going to force me. He said no one would come to my rescue. That he would make me his and I would be forced to marry him."

Beth shoved him again and jumped up from the settee. She kicked his still body that now lay slumped on the floor.

Cora saw the blood flowing from the back of his head and fear filled her. Was he dead? Had she killed him?

Had she just killed the son of a congressman? Oh no, she couldn't have.

"I think I killed him," she said, shock filling her. No, this couldn't happen. This would ruin her life.

"No, he can't be dead," Beth said, leaning over him. "He's too mean to die."

She held her hand in front of his mouth. "He's not breathing."

"He must be breathing," Cora said. "He has to be."

Beth's brown eyes grew wide and she glanced at her sister. "He's dead. He's not breathing. You killed him."

Shaking her head, Cora hit him in the chest. "Wake up. Wake up, you can't be dead. I'm not going to let you destroy me. Wake up."

How had this happened? All she'd seen was Harrison on top of Beth and she'd felt such a surge of anger to witness him compromising her sister. She couldn't let him get away with trapping her sister into marriage, but she had not meant to kill him.

Stepping over his still body, she leaned down and picked up his hand. She felt his wrist, searching for a pulse.

Nothing.

She laid her head on his chest, listening for a heartbeat.

Nothing.

"He's dead," Cora said, her voice cracking. "I killed him."

They would hang her.

The Weaver twins were well known in town and everyone would enjoy seeing them taken down. Their parents had saved their fortune during the Civil War and had been supporters of the north. Now their daughters would hang for killing a congressman's son, regardless that he was trying to molest Beth.

"What are we going to do now?"

"We need to call the sheriff," Cora said, thinking she would be spending the rest of her life in jail.

Beth reached out and grabbed her. "Sister, I can't live without you. This wasn't your fault." Her eyes teared up. "It was my fault. You kept warning me that there was something weird about him. You were right."

"I've killed him. We must speak to the law."

"But you were defending me," Beth said.

It wouldn't matter. They would never believe her. The law would be on his side. Cora would hang.

"It doesn't matter, Beth, he's the son of a congressman," she said. "They will hang me."

"Then we're going to run," Beth said. "We can just leave. We'll go out west."

Cora thought of the mail order bride ad she'd seen, in a place she had never heard of before.

Angel Creek, Montana.

"Beth, you must read this ad I saw today," she said, turning to run up the stairs to her room. She came back down with the gazette in her hand.

Her sister was staring at her like she'd lost her mind. "Why are we talking about ads when we need to run?"

Beth didn't understand, but soon she would.

"Grumpy man looking for a wife to live in the wilds of Montana. No neighbors, nearest town is miles away.

A large cattle ranch with a small log home. You've been warned."

Beth stared at her, her eyes large and wide. "Are you crazy? He doesn't want a wife."

"I don't want a husband," she replied and she didn't. Men could be such a pain, and so far, her dealings with them did not make her want to marry. "Maybe we could work out some kind of deal. We marry not for love or sex or anything, but to help each other out."

"You don't know this man," she said. "What if he's a wife-beater? We would be out in the wilds of Montana."

Beth threw back her head and moaned. "I can't believe it has come to this. You have one bad experience with a man and you decide love and marriage are not for you."

"One? Really after today, you can say one?" Cora said.

"All right, two. Montana is so far away," Beth said.

"Exactly. How could anyone find me in the mountains? I think this may be the answer to our problems," Cora said with a grin.

The law would never find her in Montana.

Shaking her head, Beth stared down at the man. "Because of this jackass, we have to leave civilization behind and start somewhere new."

"Think of it as a new adventure," Cora said, feeling excited. This town had seemed to sap all of her enthusiasm. She was ready to leave Charleston behind.

"What are we going to do with the body?"

Cora thought for a moment. "Leave it. The servants can deal with it in the morning."

A shiver went through Beth. "I'm not certain I can trust men ever again."

Laughter bubbled up from Cora. "Beth, you like men. You'll have a suitor as soon we arrive in town. Now help me carefully word my response to Mack Lawson. Maybe I should start my letter 'from a grumpy woman.'"

"That's certainly appealing. You two should be perfect for one another. A couple cantankerous souls searching for each other in the night. Good grief."

Cora didn't believe in perfect couples or even a happily ever after. That wasn't possible from what she'd seen.

This seemed like the ideal solution. A marriage of inconvenience.

# CHAPTER 3

For almost four months they had traveled by train, boat, and now a stagecoach, trying to reach the remote area of Montana. From what Cora had seen, the mountains were beautiful with pine trees reaching up to the sky and snow glistening white.

She'd been shocked when the stagecoach driver told them they had caught the last stage of the year. And yet that would make it that much more difficult to locate her. It would be spring or even summer before anyone could find her, if they did then.

The memory of the night that Harrison died made her shiver as she thought of how they had carefully chosen the things they wanted to take with them before they left early the next morning before the servants arrived.

The most harrowing time had been before the train left. She'd withdrawn all their money from the bank, sewed it up in the hem of their dresses, and then gotten on the first train to St. Louis.

Now they sat in a wooden box on the last stretch of the road. Before they left Fort Benton, they had sent Mr. Lawson a telegram, advising him they would soon arrive.

Cora only hoped he wasn't as mean as his correspondence sounded.

The stage rounded the corner, the horses suddenly eager like they knew this was the end of the journey.

Shops lined the street as the coach began to slow.

Would Mr. Lawson be waiting for them? A tremor of excitement trickled through her and she thought of his ad. Would he be a crabby old man? He'd not said his age, but he sounded old.

A church, the mercantile, and even a saloon lined the street and the little town looked bigger than the fort they had traveled through.

"Oh, sister, what have we done? Maybe we should have stayed and fought for your freedom in Charleston," Beth said, glancing out the window. "It's so small."

Beth had expressed doubts since they left, but Cora knew for certain that a jury would have found her guilty and strung her up, regardless that she'd been fighting to save Beth. Rich men could do what they wanted. Especially a carpetbagger now turned congressman whose only son she had killed.

The stage began to slow and she knew the moment of reckoning would soon be upon them.

"Remember, be nice, polite, tell him nothing about our reason for leaving."

"What if he accepts you, but not me?" Beth said. "We didn't tell him about me traveling with you."

Cora felt nervous about that as well, but she was not going to leave Beth behind in Charleston. They were sisters. They were twins and where one went, the other was at her side.

"Then we are here and have reason to get out of the contract," Cora said. "We'll find a way."

Maybe they just rented a room in Angel Creek or a small house and stayed there. Mr. Lawson was not the only man in town.

With a sigh, Beth looked out the window. "Two men are standing, watching the stage arrive. Sister, I think one of them is your man. And he's quite handsome, though he is frowning. And he's not old. I was certain you were going to be marrying a crotchety old man."

Cora tried to laugh, but she was too nervous. "Me too."

The man would be keenly disappointed if he thought she was going to marry him the moment she stepped out of the stage. She didn't know what kind of arrangements he might have made, but she would not marry him until she knew more about him. Especially after he described himself as grumpy.

The stage came to a halt and they sat there, waiting for the driver to put the steps down and open the door.

"You go first," Beth said. "I want to hang back and see his reaction."

Cora's hands clenched. She took a deep breath and released it as the door opened and she stepped out of the coach.

What was she thinking when she'd agreed to marry a man she'd never met before?

As she glanced around at their new hometown, she saw two men standing to the side whispering. Turning, she helped Beth alight from the stage.

The men began to walk toward them and her heart began to beat inside her chest. He was a young man, not old at all. Tall with broad shoulders and muscular build, his emerald eyes twinkled, a straight nose, high cheekbones, and a mouth that was full and ripe and she wanted to reach out and run her fingers along his full lip.

This was a man she could live with if he had a nice personality.

Quickly she took a deep breath and didn't say a word, waiting for him to speak first.

"Cora Weaver?" he asked stepping forward.

"Yes," she said. "And you must be the grumpy man searching for a wife?"

The man standing beside him snickered.

Mack grinned, his full lips curving. "And you must be the grumpy woman who needs a man."

"That's me," she said. "And this is my twin sister, Beth."

"I didn't know you were bringing your sister," he said.

"There was no way I would leave her behind," she said, thinking that maybe this was not the way to start out a marriage, but she didn't care.

Mack shook her hand and then the second man stepped forward.

"I'm Mack's brother James Lawson," he said. "You two look almost exactly alike. Welcome to Angel Creek."

"We are identical twins. Thank you for coming to get us," Beth said, giving James that smile she always gave when she flirted.

Good grief, her sister may be the first one to marry, the way she was flashing her eyes at him.

The stagecoach driver unloaded their trunks and the men glanced at them. "Is this everything?"

"Yes," Cora replied.

"Should we head to the courthouse?" Mack asked.

This was the moment of truth. Cora couldn't promise forever to a man she didn't know. Not even to save her life. She'd seen too much in her short life that made her think not to marry the first man who came along.

"Mr. Lawson, we don't know each other. You've already confessed to being difficult. I'm not ready to marry you just yet. Is there someplace in town we could stay until I'm ready for us to say our vows? This way if one of us decides this is not going to work, we don't have to go through a nasty divorce."

The man grinned at her and she could see he was delighted with her suggestion. Did he even want to marry?

"There will be no divorce. I think that's a fine suggestion," he said. "You can stay at the Rose Haven boarding house."

"No," James said and she turned to stare at him. Why was he interfering?

"We live way out of town. The only way to get to know each other is for you to be staying at the ranch. Ms. Hattie, our housekeeper, lives with us. She can serve as a chaperone."

Cora bit her lip and then turned to her sister. They had already had to face one man trying to force himself on them, she wasn't about to experience it a second time. After all, she'd killed a man to protect her sister and she didn't want to have to do so again.

"We'll need our own separate bedroom," Cora said.

Mack reached out and touched her on the arm. "It's getting late and it will take us about two hours to reach the ranch. You and Beth can sleep in the guest room. Hattie has her own quarters in the house. I'm in no hurry to marry either, so this will work out perfectly. I give you my word that you and Beth will be well chaperoned."

For some reason, Cora believed him. He didn't appear to be mean and spiteful or even grumpy, and for that, she was glad. But they still had a lot to work out before she would ever agree to marry Mr. Lawson.

She glanced at Beth who was smiling at James. Good grief, once again her sister was flirting and she could see the attraction between her and James. She would have to be on guard, watching her every move. The woman just didn't learn.

"Beth, is that all right with you?"

She turned and glanced at her sister. "Of course. I'm just glad we're here."

Cora turned back to Mack. "All right, as long as we have a chaperone."

"Then let's load up the wagon and get going, so we can get home before dark. I've got extra blankets in the wagon in case you get cold."

With a shiver, Cora realized she was cold standing in the bright sunshine with nothing but a shawl wrapped around her. In Charleston, a heavy winter coat was seldom needed.

"In a few days, we'll need to come back to town and buy you and Beth some winter clothing. Montana gets mighty cold."

That was the one thing Cora had not considered. The cold. The snow and coming from Charleston, they were ill prepared. No gloves, no long johns, not even a heavy coat.

"Good," she said.

Mack reached out and took her hand and placed it in the crook of his elbow. "Are you ready to go to the ranch?"

It was then that Cora realized how different her life

would be. Living out of town, no neighbors, no shops, only the ranch. But that would keep her safe.

"Yes," she said, gazing into his emerald eyes, liking the way they sparkled.

The man didn't appear anything like what she'd read into his ad. And yet there was something about him she felt drawn to.

Maybe she was making the biggest mistake of her life, or maybe this was the new beginning she needed. Whatever it was, she was willing to take it to stay safe.

# CHAPTER 4

*M*ack had been shocked when someone answered his ad. And now he was in awe at the gorgeous woman as he helped her up into the wagon. How in hell's name had he gotten so lucky?

Dark brunette hair, brown eyes, a full mouth that needed kissing. Those lips were just begging for him to show her how a man kissed a woman. And curves into next week. What was wrong with her that she'd never found someone to marry her?

Yes, she had a twin sister and already he could see his brother had set his intentions on her. What would it be like for the two men to marry sisters? Two women who looked so much alike.

He'd have to speak to James later when they were alone. Ask him if he felt comfortable with this situation.

Thank goodness, he'd brought several throws with him and he tucked the woman into the wagon on the seat next to him. He handed his brother a throw blanket and his brother did the same with Beth.

"If you're still cold, I'll give you my jacket," he told her as he climbed up onto the seat beside her. Their hips were touching and he liked the feeling.

When everyone was settled, he clicked to the horses. "It'll take us about two hours to reach the ranch."

She nodded and again he wondered why a beautiful woman like herself would not have a husband. In Angel Creek, she would have more suiters lined up than she could handle.

"What is the name of your ranch, Mr. Lawson," she said as the wagon began to roll. Wouldn't gossip be swirling through town tonight. Mack and James Lawson took two beauties home.

"Lawson Creek," he said. "No, it's not original, but that's what my father named the place. It will do. And please call me Mack. And I would like to call you Cora."

"You may," she said. "Tell me, Mack, why did you write your ad that way?"

He laughed. "Because I didn't want to advertise for a wife and my brother made me. You see I really didn't want to remarry."

"Remarry? You never mentioned you'd been married before."

"I'm a widower," he said, trying to erase the look of concern on her face.

"Any children?"

"No," he said, remembering the baby that Margery

had lost. Sometimes he wondered if that was what had her scrambling to find a way into town and leave him and the memories behind.

They had both been devastated. She'd carried their son for seven months before she miscarried. So close and they'd been so excited about their first child. Feeling the sadness well up inside him, he pushed the thoughts from his mind.

Today was a new beginning. One he didn't want, but it was looking better and better.

They were silent for a moment as the wagon rolled down Main Street past the saloon, the church, the mercantile, and then past the edge of town.

"Why didn't you want to marry again?"

The real reason he wasn't quite ready to share with her. It was not something he told just anyone. Some things were private.

"For now, let's just say she was not who I thought she was," he said. "We'll talk more later. Why did you answer my ad?" he asked.

A strange expression crossed her face and then she glanced at him and smiled. "Yours was the most interesting." She laughed. "What man admits he's grumpy? My biggest fear was arriving to an old man. Or someone mean. Are you mean, Mr. Lawson?"

"No, but I can become quite irritated."

"You can say that again," his brother said from the back of the wagon.

"Life is not always easy," he admitted. "Sometimes I can get testy."

"We all do. As long as you're not mean, I can handle anything else, but I will not accept a man who would hit or beat me or mistreat me in any way."

Turning, he faced her. He'd never considered that a woman would think he would beat her. That would never happen.

The horse knew the way home, the pine trees lined the road on either side. Montana was cold and beautiful, and there was no place else that Mack would ever live.

"No decent man would hit a woman," he said, glancing at her. "You will never have to fear being beaten or hit by me."

The question made him angry. Not that he was upset with her, but rather the thought of a man hurting a woman. It was wrong.

"Thank you for telling me. That's a relief. I guess, I'll just have to witness your temper in action." She gazed at him, her lips curled in a small smile. "I'm actually quite pleased."

"Me too," he said. "But why hasn't some man snatched you up and married you?"

A woman as beautiful as Cora would have a bevy of suitors. Why had she turned them down?

"Oh, look, Beth, isn't the scenery pretty?"

Did she just avoid his question?

"Yes," she said with a giggle.

Why did he get the feeling she was stalling? Why did men not like the woman?

"Hmm, the lady isn't answering my question."

She shrugged. "The lady is picky. And men can be fickle. Before the war, I wasn't old enough to court. After the war, many of the men did not return. Currently, the city is filled with scalawags and men I would never even consider. The men who did return seemed broken."

So the lady was either hard to get along with or persnickety or so picky no one wanted her. Only time would tell which. Mack had not considered the mental state of men returning from the war and it was true. War did horrible things to everyone involved. Suddenly he wondered how the war had affected her. What scars had been left behind?

"Did you leave family and friends?"

"Our family is dead. Our friends are scattered. It was time for a change. I'd been in Charleston all my life and the city is just not the same as it was before the war. Beth and I decided it was time to leave."

That made sense. In Montana, they had avoided the war since they were not a state and he'd felt like it wasn't really his fight. So James and he had worked on building their ranch. After hearing of so much bloodshed, they were glad they stayed home.

"Tell me about your ranch. I'm a city girl and I know nothing about living on a ranch."

This was his reason for not wanting to marry. This

was what frightened him about Cora. He'd already experienced one woman who didn't know how to live on a ranch. A tightness gripped his chest. Margery leaving had almost killed him. He couldn't do it again.

If he gave Cora his heart and she decided to leave, he would be more than devastated this time. This time, it would kill him. He couldn't go through this with another woman. Somehow he would need to convince his brother to send Cora and Beth back.

With a sigh, he told her about Lawson's Creek. "My father started the ranch, and for the last twenty years, we've been growing every year. This year more than ever."

"Almost fifty new calves," James spoke up from the back of the wagon. "In another year, our herd should double in size if we can keep the wolves from stealing the calves."

Cora's head jerked toward the back. "Wolves?"

"Oh yes, we have coyote, wolves, bear, and deer."

The woman licked her lips nervously and already Mack was worried she was going to run. At least if she did before they married, he wouldn't be as hurt. But he could not suffer the humiliation of a second wife bolting on him.

"You don't have coyotes, wolves, and bears in Charleston?"

"No," she said, her eyes large and filled with fear. "The most dangerous animal in town is the scalawag or the carpetbagger, though most of them have disappeared in the last six months."

He couldn't help himself as he started to laugh.

"Those are people," he said.

"Yes, who can be just as dangerous if not more than wild animals."

"True," he said. "Do you know how to use a weapon?"

"Of course not," Cora. "Though I have been known to be quite handy with the fireplace poker."

Beth choked, sitting in the back of the wagon.

"You all right, darling," James asked.

Oh, great she'd already become *darling*. Not even ten miles out of town and his brother was already smitten.

"Yes," she said and gave a little giggle.

The sun was beginning to set, the rays reflecting off the mountains.

"Are your sunsets this pretty in Charleston?" Mack asked.

"No, they're not," she said gazing about. "That's beautiful the way the orange makes the mountains glow."

At least she appreciated beauty, but how would she handle being stuck away from town for months at a time?

"We're getting close to the ranch," he told her. "Our land starts here at the marker. We have about four hundred acres."

Her mouth fell open and suddenly he realized maybe he shouldn't have told her that. If she was just after their money, she'd be sorely disappointed. They were land rich and cash poor. Hopefully soon that would all change.

"How many head of cattle do you have?" she asked.

Really he had no idea. He knew at roundup when they sold some of their cattle, but the animals kept them busy.

"A lot," he answered, thinking that was probably better she didn't know an exact number.

"Plus, we have horses, chickens, and goats," James said. "In the winter, we're busy working in the barn, putting out bales of hay for the cattle. But in the summer, we're riding the range, sorting cattle, and repairing fences. It's our busiest time."

They rode along for a few more minutes. "When do you have trouble with the bears and wolves?"

Mack glanced at her and smiled. "The wolves and the coyotes are year-round, but the bears are hibernating now."

"Has a bear ever attacked you?"

"No," Mack said. "As long as you don't get between the mother and her cubs, they usually run off."

The woman's face seemed to relax. "Fighting wild animals is not why I came to Montana. Beth and I wanted a different life. We never considered coyotes and wolves."

For some reason, he expected her to say a life of love and family, but she didn't and he thought that was weird.

"What do you want in a husband?"

That was a question he often asked of young ladies and he was always surprised at the answer.

She tilted her head and thought for a moment. "A man who is respected. Someone who treats me in a way that shows everyone I'm his wife and his friend."

Mack contemplated what she said. She didn't mention love. The woman must be a virgin for her not to consider it important. But every girl knew that with marriage came sex. Why was she avoiding the question?

"What about your husband being your lover?" he asked as he gazed at her.

"Not important," she said as he stared at her in awkward silence.

"Well, that's a problem," he said and her brows raised as she stared at him.

"I don't believe in love," she told him. "I've never seen it."

Stunned, he stared at her in awe. "Not even your parents?"

She laughed. "Especially not my parents. I've never been in love. I don't think I ever will be."

How did a man with trust issues, who didn't really want to marry, show a woman love? They were about as mismatched as a cat and a dog. Already he could hear the howling in his ears as they chased one another. This was definitely going to be a challenge. And he did like a good challenge.

# CHAPTER 5

*A*s the wagon pulled up in front of the house, Cora was shocked at the beauty of the place. Pine trees lined the road, and while it was dark when they arrived, the house was so beautifully constructed of logs with smoke drifting up from the fireplace. Almost like a painting.

Nothing like this in Charleston.

A woman in an apron stood waiting for them on the porch, waving furiously at them.

After Mack set the brake on the wagon, he jumped out and came around to help her out.

He placed his hands on her waist as he lifted her out of the wagon. Her breasts brushed against his chest as he set her down, her breath fast and shallow. Her feet sank into cold wet snow.

Ugh. They would need boots. Real boots.

Glancing around, she saw a barn not far from the

house with a small chicken coop on the outside and an animal pen in front of the barn.

She and Beth had always lived in the city and she realized this was going to be a whole new experience.

A glow in the darkness was all that was left of the sun. Tilting her head back, she glanced up at the heavens. "Oh my, look at the stars. There are so many of them."

With the lights of the city, it was hard to see the stars. Sure, she missed her childhood home, but there were not many happy memories there, so she felt no remorse in leaving.

All she wanted was a new beginning and this looked like a great opportunity.

"Wait until there is a full moon," Mack said. Taking her hand, he led her up the front porch to the woman who was their housekeeper.

"Ladies, I didn't know there was going to be two of you. Welcome to Lawson's Creek. I'm Hattie."

"We're sisters," Cora said. "Twins."

"Oh dear," she said with a laugh. "Were you expecting this, Mack?"

"No, but we'll make do," he said, nodding his head to James who had carried Beth from the wagon and set her on the porch.

"Thank you, kind sir," she said, batting her dark brown eyes at him. Beth made up for Cora's lack of flirting. Sometimes it was too much as Cora turned her attention back to the house.

Cora was in awe of the place. As Mack opened the door, she heard a howling noise and froze.

"Coyotes," Mack said. "Don't worry, they're a long way off."

A shudder rippled through her at the sound of the lonely cry. She stepped into the living area of the home. The room was gorgeous with high ceilings, large beams holding up the ceiling, a big rock fireplace with a roaring fire set into the back wall. The smell of something delicious floated through the house.

"How was the wedding?" Hattie asked.

They all looked at each other.

"We decided to wait," Cora said. "Before I can promise forever, I need to know who I'm marrying."

The woman smiled. "Smart."

"I hope you don't mind being our chaperone?"

"Not at all," she said. "This will give you some time to get to know one another."

All Cora knew was that most men didn't really seem to like her and she wanted to give Mack a chance to back out. Why they didn't like her, she didn't know, but she was not one for flirting. Someone in their family had to be the practical one and the job had always fallen to her. Even when their mother was alive.

"Let me show you to your bedroom. You ladies can wash up and then we'll have dinner. I prepared a special dinner because I thought it would be your wedding feast, but it can be your arriving at Lawson's Creek feast.

We're thrilled you're here," Hattie said, leading the way to the bedroom.

Cora glanced back to make certain Beth was coming, but she was talking to James. Mack must be unloading their trunks because he was nowhere in sight.

"Beth," Cora called.

Her sister looked up at her and she motioned for her to follow.

"See you at dinner," Beth said with a giggle.

At home, she and Beth had not shared a room. It was going to be difficult to have to listen to her sister's giggles. Part of her still believed they could not be in Montana, if only Beth had chosen her suitors more carefully.

Harrison Dane was a man who had a great background but was a cruel man in reality. A man that Cora had killed. A shudder rippled up her spine, she never had believed she was capable of murder, but she had no choice. And she'd only meant to knock him out.

Saving Beth had been her intention, but that was now all in the past. Better not to dwell on how she'd killed a man.

"This is where you ladies will sleep," Hattie said, gazing at Cora. Beth had yet to arrive. "The men are sleeping on the other side of the house and my quarters are in the middle. So no one should question that you girls are not being properly chaperoned. And I will be watching."

Cora didn't care. She would not be making any trips

down to Mack's or James's bedroom and neither would Beth. She'd make certain.

"Thank you, Hattie," she said. "I need to make certain this is right for both of us before I say I do."

The woman smiled at her. "Thank you. I've been worried about Mack since I learned he had put that ad in the paper. His first marriage ended so tragically. I didn't want him to get hurt a second time."

Mack had secrets he hadn't shared with her, but then, so did she. She had not decided yet whether she would tell him that she had murdered a man. But she was curious about his first wife.

"How did his first wife die?" Cora asked.

The woman's brows raised. "That is for him to tell you, not me. It's not something he likes to talk about, so give him some time. While you two are getting to know each other, I'm sure he'll tell you all about Margery."

Beth breezed in through the door. "We're sharing a room? We haven't done that since we were babies."

Hattie turned on her. "We didn't expect two women and there are only four bedrooms in the house. You'll have to share for now. Dinner will be served in ten minutes. I'd suggest you wash up and come to the dining room."

The woman whirled around and left the room.

"Well, she certainly didn't like my comment about sharing a room," Beth said, sinking down on the bed. She removed her hat she'd worn all the way from Charleston. "Isn't James handsome. I feared I was going to be a third wheel, but frankly, I think I like him better than Mack."

What could Cora say? She'd half expected Beth to step into her shoes and marry Mack, but then when she'd seen he had a brother, she knew exactly what Beth would do.

"Good," Cora said, going to the pitcher and water bowl. She poured the water into the basin then picked up soap and lathered her hands. "Let's just wait and see how the next few days go." After she finished washing, she picked up a towel and dried her hands.

"Did you see that town?" Beth said. "Oh my, it was maybe the size of one long city block in Charleston. Life is certainly very different here. Wonder what they do for fun?"

"Count cows," Cora said with a laugh. "Come on, it's time for dinner and you're already on Hattie's bad side."

The girl scooted off the bed and came to the water bowl and pitcher. "Do you think we're going to like living here?"

"Yes," Cora said. "We have to like living here because we cannot return to Charleston."

Beth sighed. "I'm going to miss the lights of the city and the harbor. I love to look at the ocean."

"The mountain sunsets are beautiful. Get used to it, Beth. We're never going back to Charleston. This is home."

# CHAPTER 6

*A*fter the ladies followed Hattie into the house, Mack turned on his brother. "She's another Margery. She's not going to like living on a ranch."

James stopped and stared at his brother. "You're not giving her a chance. If you compare every woman to Margery, you'll never remarry."

"That's what I was trying to do," Mack said. "I never planned on getting married a second time. Too much heartache. Too much grief." Unhitching the horses from the wagon, Mack rose and shook his head. "This was a mistake. I think you should offer to return them to town and put them on the next stage back to the fort."

James chuckled. "Can't. This was the last run of the stage until spring. They're stuck here until the big thaw. Besides, it's just an excuse for you to get out of marrying Cora."

Mack sighed. He'd forgotten this was the last stage.

There was no train and the only other way out of town was by horse. Unless, of course, you had money or power. Then you could certainly buy your way through the mountains. These ladies didn't seem to be the kind of women who rode horses. If they stayed, that would have to change. Everyone was needed at the roundup, including the women.

"I'm not marrying her if I don't think it will work. It really pleased me that she felt the same way," he said, thinking that was a plus for the woman.

He removed the harness from around the horse's neck and lead it to the barn, his brother following.

"You're being too cautious," his brother warned. "If you want this to work, you need to court her."

"She's here in my house. How do I do that?"

As they put the horses in their stalls, his brother's brows drew together. "Something different, unique."

"Well, that sounds like a great idea, but I don't have a clue as to what. It's not like I can write her a sonnet or take her on a picnic."

"Why not? Why can't you write her a sonnet?"

"Because I'm a cowboy who doesn't write poetry."

His brother grinned. "Then write her a note each morning and tell her something that you like about her. Why not take her on a picnic? Why not take her riding around the ranch? Beth told me her sister has been hurt by men, you two share some things in common and you might be able to work something out."

There was only one major problem with his brother's plan. "The woman is afraid of coyotes."

"Smart woman," his brother said.

"You and I both know we've had to learn to live with the wildlife around here. We have learned to adapt to the land. I've already had one wife who couldn't do it; what if she's just like Margery?"

"Stop! If she were Margery, she'd be dead." His brother commanded. "You have compared her to Margery multiple times now, and if you do that to her, you might as well take her into town and tell the bachelors there that she's on the market."

Mack released a heavy sigh. James was right. The woman deserved a chance and he had her tagged as just another Margery.

"You're right. I'll stop doing that," he said. "But I reserve the right to still be concerned."

James shook his head. "Damn, you're a stubborn, grumpy man who I would never marry."

"Well, thank God for that," Mack said.

They finished brushing the horses and gave them their feed.

"What do you think of Beth?" James asked.

There was so much he would like to comment on but knew better than to discourage his brother regarding a woman. It was best if he kept his opinions to himself.

"She's young. She's beautiful and friendly and you two were getting along very nicely."

A little too nicely as far as Mack was concerned, but that was not really his business.

"Yeah, we may be married by Christmas."

The memory of his parents' happy marriage washed over Mack. That's what he wanted, and he thought James wanted the same thing. The pit of his stomach seemed to tighten as he remembered his first marriage. Quickly he pushed it out of his mind.

If he married Cora, this time would be different. It had to be.

"Just remember that marriage is forever, so whoever you choose, be certain of her."

His brother frowned and he glanced back at him. "You're one to be talking. Married a young woman who had no business being married and you brought her to the ranch."

"And that's why I'm being so cautious this time," he said. "Hopefully, I've learned from my mistakes."

They walked out of the barn and toward the house. Snowflakes were gently falling from the sky.

"Going to be a cold one tonight," Mack said. "A good test of the women's fortitude in living on a ranch."

"Christmas is only five weeks away. We already have snow on the ground."

"Yes, we do," Mack said. "Wonder if the women will want to decorate for Christmas. Remember how Ma used to decorate the house? We should get down the old decorations and put up a tree."

His brother glanced at him and smiled. "You never want to decorate."

"I'm trying to do better," Mack said. "You could help me by not pointing out things like I never want to decorate."

"You and Cora could go cut a Christmas tree in the next week. That might be one of your courting times."

It was a thought. It was still a little early, but that would give them some time alone to talk and get to know each other.

But tomorrow morning, he was going to leave her a message. He liked the idea of surprising her with special thoughts first thing in the morning. That he could do. Sonnets were out. Besides she didn't appear to be the type of woman who would want rhymes from him. That would be more like her sister.

Mack was trying not to get excited about Cora, but there was something about her that interested him. Could she be the right woman for him?

# CHAPTER 7

The next morning, Cora awoke to the sun shining brightly in the bedroom window. Usually she was up before the sun rose, but this morning, she'd slept in and she felt certain that Mack would believe she was a lazy person.

Jumping up from the bed, she noticed her sister had already dressed and left the room. Only Cora remained in bed.

Quickly, she opened her trunk and found a dress that was more of a house dress than a fancy traveling dress.

She gazed about the room and realized that Beth had already removed some of her clothes from her trunk and taken over the counter with her brush and hair clips. With a sigh, Cora brushed out her hair and then decided to let the dark curls flow down her back.

Ready for the day, when she opened the door, there

SYLVIA MCDANIEL

was a folded piece of paper on the door with her name on the outside.

She pulled the note from the door and unfolded it.

*Dearest Cora,*

*I'm in a really great mood today, so I promise to be extremely nice to you. The weather is chilly, but the sun is shining. Would you care to go on a tour of the ranch with me? I'd like to get to know you better. Already, I can tell you that I really like the way your brown eyes gaze at me and I can almost tell what you're feeling from the way they darken. Let's spend some time alone, just you and me.*

*Mack*

A smile spread across her face. Should she trust him and go alone with the man to see his ranch?

What if after he showed her this life, she didn't like it? What would she do then?

With a sigh, she went to the kitchen where she heard talking. When she walked in, they all glanced up at her.

"Sorry, I slept so long. I haven't done that in years," she said, sitting at the table.

Mack smiled at her. "You must have been tired. That was no easy trip coming across the country."

It had been a horrendous trip and she never wanted to do it again and yet she feared she might have to. Especially if the sheriff learned where she was. The law would take her back to Charleston.

She lowered her eyes and then gazed at Mack. "I'd enjoy spending some time today seeing the ranch."

A grin spread across his face. "Great. Eat breakfast and then we can leave. I'll go hitch the wagon."

"And thanks for the note," she said. "I liked it. It was nice, not grumpy at all."

"You're welcome," he grinned. "You eat your breakfast and then we'll go."

Rising, he gave her a smile then hurried out the door. She kind of hated that he was gone, but she knew he was busy preparing.

"What are you going to do?" she asked Beth.

"Oh, I'll find something to keep me busy. Hattie is going to show me how to collect eggs."

James grinned at Beth, and Cora didn't think Hattie would be showing Beth, but rather James.

Tonight she would warn Beth and remind her why they were here. The girl had to learn to be more careful around men. They were dangerous.

Thirty minutes later, Mack was helping her into the wagon and putting blankets around her. He'd given her a long coat to wear. She smelled him on the piece of clothing.

The manly scent was nice and she took a deep breath and felt her insides quiver. That was different.

"Are you ready?" he asked as he climbed up beside her and spread the blanket over their legs.

They were sitting hip to hip in the wagon and their bodies touched at the shoulder. She couldn't remember the last time she'd been this close to a man and then she remembered the soldier and she shuddered.

When a man is told no, sometimes they tried to convince the woman to change her mind. Beth and she had sent the man sailing out the door. No wonder they were called the crazy Weaver twins.

"Are you cold?" he asked.

"No, I'm fine," she replied and knew that if this was going to work, she would need to tell him so many things. Why did it seem like her life around men had never been great?

When he clicked to the horses, the wagon moved through the yard. "We got a little snow overnight. Not much. If you decide to marry me, you have to realize that in January and February we don't leave the house. The weather is nasty, so we don't go into town."

That surprised her. "What if you need supplies?"

"That's why we have a large root cellar for cold things and Hattie will show you the closet where the canned goods are stored. In the summer, Hattie raises a vegetable garden and she cans."

Canning was something Cora had always wanted to learn. "Do you think she'll show me how? I'd love to learn."

Mack's head jerked as he turned to stare at her. "I'm sure she would love to. It's a big job and she gets so tired when she cans."

A smile flittered across Cora's face. "Good. I have wanted to grow my own vegetables and can for so long. During the war, food became so scarce, and it would have been good if we had our own food source."

With a sigh, she gazed at the beautiful countryside. "Where are the cattle? They aren't in the trees are they?"

"No, there is a valley we're coming up to soon where we keep them in the winter. It's closer to the house and we can feed them if the snow gets too bad or even bring them up to the house. Two years ago, we brought them up to the field right behind the barn. The blizzards were so strong and this way we could feed them hay right there."

Their winters were a lot longer and stronger than anything they ever experienced in Charleston.

They rode along and suddenly a valley appeared before them and there were hundreds of cattle eating bits of grass through the snow and the hay that was scattered about the field.

"Wow, that's a lot of cattle," she said.

"Yes," he replied, picking up her hand. He brought it to his mouth and kissed the back of it.

She tensed and yet warmth flowed through her. She liked the feel of his lips on her hand.

He said, "Something you said yesterday has bothered me."

"What?"

"You said you didn't believe in love. Why?"

With a sigh, she gazed out at the animals mindlessly eating. Not everyone experienced love.

"Several reasons. My parents for one. My father only wanted my mother because she was from a well-known family in Charleston that had hit hard times. He married her to bring prestige to his name, but all he did was bring humiliation to my mother. How can you love a man who drank himself into oblivion every night? He made a lot of money off the railroad, so he left us wealthy. I would have taken a happy family life over the money anytime."

"I'm sorry," Mack said.

"The reason I want to make certain that we're right for one another is because of my father. If I had been my mother, I would have kicked him out the door years ago. But she put up with him until he killed them both in a buggy accident."

His fingers rubbed the back of her hand in a soothing manner and she gazed at him. "When I started courting, I quickly learned that many men were the same. I courted a man named Jerome who I thought was different, but come to find out, he was just like my father. A drunk. I'm sorry, but for me to marry you, you're going to have to prove to me that you're a good man."

That was not even telling him about Harrison. Her luck with men had been dismal. Dismal enough that she was distrustful.

"I don't believe in love because I truly have never seen love between a man and a woman."

A smile crossed his face. "I like a good challenge. Your father drank too much. I've never been a big drinker. Occasionally, I like a sip of whiskey with my eggnog, but I never want to be incapacitated in case of an emergency on the ranch. So I have one glass and that's all. What did the other man do that made you distrust men?"

She could tell that Mack was a man who liked to be in control. In the day they had known each other, she saw he liked to be in charge of the way things were done and she was fine with that. As long as he wasn't a drunk.

"Jerome liked women and strong drink," she said. "It seemed like I was not enough for him. He needed more than one woman at a time. So I ended my relationship with him. Since then, I've avoided men. You're the first in a long time."

Mack clicked to the horses and the wagon began to roll again. "You know, Cora, we have a lot in common. I've not been a big fan of women for the last five years. It was why I said *grumpy* in my ad. If I had my way, not one woman would have answered. And yet here you are and I'm glad you're here."

The horse shook his head and made a guttural noise. "Yes, Cinnamon, I know it's time for lunch."

She giggled at the idea of a horse telling its owner it was time to eat.

"Why don't you like marriage?"

"Because like you, my wife decided I was not what she wanted. She ran away with a peddler that showed up at the ranch. After she died, I hated what she'd done to me. It was then I decided I would never marry again. But my brother had other ideas."

They were both victims of people who had hurt

them. No wonder neither one of them wanted to marry. No wonder they were leery of each other and found it hard to trust, and yet somehow, she knew she needed to learn to depend on Mack if she was going to stay here.

"Why did you say you like a challenge? Do you consider me a challenge?"

A grin spread across his face and he pulled the wagon to a halt. "Look out at the valley. Have you ever seen a more beautiful sight?"

Turning, she stared and her mouth opened in awe. The colors of the mountains were gorgeous, though the temperature was a mite cold. A shiver rippled through her and he pulled her closer to him.

His hand turned her cheek to face him and he stared at her. "You're a very intriguing and challenging woman. I've not been interested in anyone for well over five years. Our situations make it very hard to trust anyone and my biggest fear is you getting bored with the ranch and wanting to leave."

What the man didn't understand was that she could never return to Charleston unless she wanted to swing from a rope.

"I'm not going anywhere," she said confidently.

"What if you never fall in love with me?" he asked.

"Like I said, I don't believe in love. I've never been around people who are in love, so I don't know what it would feel like," she said.

Leaning toward her, his hand reached out and pulled her even closer. "Again, challenge accepted. If we marry, it's important to me that you fall in love with me, and me with you. My parents' marriage was a shining example of the kind of love that I want. A happy home where my father honored my mother. A place where neither one worried about the other cheating because there was so much love between them. A home where they raised me and James and buried two more children."

With a sigh, he closed his eyes. "Their lives were not easy, but in times of crisis, they had each other. They loved one another and they faced life together. That's the kind of love I want to share with a woman."

It sounded like a wonderful life and a little piece of hope began to grow inside her. Could Mack be the man she'd been looking for all her life? Was he the man she'd dreamed of as a young girl?

As he opened his eyes, he stared into hers and then he leaned into her. "I'm going to kiss you. Because if there are no sparks between us, then we're just wasting each other's time."

"Sparks?"

A grin spread across his face as his lips covered hers. At first, she was startled, but then she began to relax in his arms. A warmth spread through her as his lips took control, moving over hers, demanding she surrender as his tongue pressed between her lips. With a gasp, she broke the kiss, her breathing sounded harsh in her ears.

"Well, that answers that question," he said. "There are

plenty of sparks between us. Enough to start a blaze. Did you feel them?"

What could she say? When she couldn't catch her breath and a warmth spread through her body.

"Yes, I felt them," she finally said. "All the way to my toes."

Mack leaned back and laughed. "You're a very honest woman and I appreciate that about you. You'll always let me know when I'm doing good and when I'm doing bad."

"Or anything in between," she said. "But that's not love."

"No, it's not love, but I think it can lead to love," he said, picking up the reins. "But can we both learn to trust again?"

# CHAPTER 8

*E*arly the next morning, Mack put yet another note on Cora's door. The message made him smile as he hurried out the door to feed the animals. Already, he could smell frying bacon and knew Hattie was busy fixing breakfast.

After taking Cora around the ranch yesterday, he felt a little better about their odds of marrying. Neither one of them trusted the other, and until they had that trust, he would never consider marrying her. And he didn't believe she would agree to marry him if there was not this bond of trust between them.

And love. But that was going to be the toughest one since Cora had never experienced the emotion.

With a jaunt in his step, he hurried across the yard to the barn.

Today, James was taking Beth out in the wagon to tour the ranch. Last night after they returned, the

SYLVIA MCDANIEL

women had helped Hattie with dinner. Then they sat in front of the fire, the four of them talking about their life in Charleston and the life here at the ranch.

When he walked Cora to her bedroom door, he'd kissed her on the cheek. It was a simple gesture, but she smiled at him and told him goodnight. It was progress and that was all he could ask for.

Quickly he fed the horses and gave them water. When all of the animals were taken care of, he walked out of the barn. A loud squawking noise came from the hen house and he turned to see what was causing the commotion.

Opening the door to the enclosure, he had to smile. Cora was shaking her finger at the orneriest hen they had in the house. "Don't bite me. I'm your friend. Or if you continue, I'll make certain you wind up in the pot. The cooking pot," she told the hen.

As she stuck her hand beneath her to take the egg, the hen struck a second time.

A screech came from Cora as she yanked her hand back. "You're going to make a nice dinner."

Mack couldn't contain his laughter another second.

She turned and glared at him.

"I'm certainly glad you're enjoying this hen attacking me," she said. "I've done all of the other hens, but this one chicken has declared war on me. She's messing with the wrong person."

Mack knew how this hen liked her eggs to be removed. She was an odd animal, as he slipped his hand

52

in from the side and pulled out the egg she was sitting on.

"If you don't succeed the first time, then try from a different angle. She didn't mind it when I go in at the side," he told her, showing her how to grab the egg and then get out of the way.

He dropped the egg into her basket and gazed at her. "Are you done?"

"Yes, I can now go back in the house and give these to Hattie," she said.

As they walked along, he picked up her hand.

"You're not feeling grumpy this morning?"

A smile crossed his face. "Not yet. How about you? Has that nasty hen made you snippy?"

"Not yet," she said. "She's going to make a fine chicken soup."

Mack couldn't help but laugh at the determination on her face. He wondered why a woman who had a bad experience courting a man would suddenly take a chance on becoming a mail-order bride. It didn't make sense.

She would be taking a chance on a man she'd never met. Especially one that claimed to be grumpy.

"Cora, why did you answer my ad? Why would someone who courted a man who was a womanizer take a chance on an ad in the *Mail Order Bride Gazette*?"

She turned and frowned at him. "Now I am feeling snippy."

"Sorry, but I have to understand, and after what you

told me yesterday, I started to question why you would take such a risk."

The snow crunched beneath their shoes as they walked from the barn back to the house.

"I've already told you that we needed to leave Charleston. There was nothing for us there and Beth likes to flirt and she was starting to get quite the reputation," Cora said, not looking at him, but walking toward the house.

Beth was quite the flirt. "Why didn't she become the mail order bride?"

"She didn't want to leave. She didn't want to marry a stranger, but then neither did I," Cora said. "And thus the reason that we're learning about each other."

Mack had not wanted to like Cora, but every minute they were together, he found her more and more fascinating. More and more, he wanted to learn all her secrets and soon marry her.

But not everything seemed to be adding up with regards to them coming out to Montana. Something felt off and he didn't understand why he felt this way, but after Margery, he paid attention when his senses detected something not quite right.

"So you dragged poor Beth to Montana," he said.

"We're twins and where one goes, so goes the other. I know how she's feeling, what she's thinking and our bodies are so alike. I know it's weird, but that's what makes us unique."

When they reached the steps leading up to the house,

he took her elbow to make certain she wouldn't slip and fall.

"I think James is taking Beth on a tour of the ranch today."

Her brown eyes flickered up and gazed at him, and for a second, he thought he saw concern. What was she hiding?

"That is such a nice drive," she said. "I'm sure she'll enjoy seeing the sights."

They were silent as they reached the deck of the house and turned to watch the sun peek over the eastern horizon. "Sunrises and sunsets are so beautiful here."

"I have a question for you," she said, turning just as the sun crested the horizon, bathing her in the early morning light. "Why did your wife want to leave you? What was wrong in your marriage?"

The woman had been thinking about what he told her and now he could see she had questions. Questions he wasn't quite ready to confide in her, but he'd give her the short version.

"She hated living on the ranch, and after she lost our baby, she was never the same."

He watched as Cora's mouth dropped open and she stared at him.

"No, life was not always good between us. That's why I want to make certain you like living miles from town with no nearby neighbors. It will always be just us, the ranch hands, and my brother."

"And children," she said.

"And eventually children," he said, thinking of the babies buried in the family cemetery alongside his parents—two baby girls and his own son. Life could be cruel.

While she had answered his question about becoming a mail-order bride, it still didn't seem to satisfy the questions he had.

"If there were other reasons why you left Charleston, I'd like to hear them."

Her eyes widened and he knew there was something else that had sent her running to Angel Creek.

"You can tell me."

A smile that didn't reach her terrified eyes crossed her face. "Right now, I have to deliver the eggs to Hattie and make sure Beth is roused from bed."

With that, she turned and entered the house. A strangely tender feeling squeezed his heart as he watched her go.

He liked Cora, but even with every reason she'd given him for leaving Charleston, it didn't seem to add up. There was something she was hiding and he was determined to find out what.

Maybe James should talk to Beth. She didn't seem quite as stubborn as Cora. Beth appeared more open and carefree than her sister.

Mack turned to the shed where James would be hitching the wagon.

When he walked into the building, his brother was

loading the wagon up with a basket of food, wine, and even a blanket.

"What are you planning on doing up in the woods?" he asked James.

The man looked up and grinned. "Spending some time getting to know Beth. While I know you and Cora are not getting hitched any time soon, I think Beth and I are doing very well. I didn't order a mail order bride, but I'm so glad she came with Cora."

Mack nodded. It was true, James and Beth were doing wonderful while he and Cora were struggling.

"I have a favor to ask you. See if you can get Beth to tell you why they left Charleston. Maybe I'm just uncertain, but I get the feeling that Cora is not telling me everything about Charleston. And I want to know before I agree to marry."

James pulled the horses in front of the wagon and began to hitch them up to the wooden vehicle.

"All right," he said. "I was planning on today being more about having fun, but I'll try to sneak in some serious time as well."

"Good," Mack said. "And thanks for the idea about the notes. I think Cora is really enjoying receiving a message from me each morning."

His brother grinned as he stepped up into the wagon. "Thanksgiving is next week, and while we don't celebrate it in Montana, they do on the East Coast. I think we should celebrate it here with the girls. Let them know we're thinking of them."

"I'll talk to Hattie today about us cooking up a big meal on Thanksgiving day."

The horses were now hitched to the wagon and Mack pulled open the doors to the barn for James. With a snap of the reins, the two horses pulled out into the morning sunshine.

"Enjoy your day with Beth," Mack said. "And I can't wait to hear what you learn."

# CHAPTER 9

*L*ate that afternoon, Beth and James returned. Beth's lips were swollen and there was a tinge of pink on her face from the sun when she walked into the house.

"Hello," she called as Cora stepped up behind her.

She jumped.

"You didn't have to scare me," she said.

"I didn't mean to," Cora said.

Beth took her by the arm and put her fingers to her lips. "Come with me."

Her sister led her into the bedroom and shut the door.

"James was asking me questions about why we left Charleston," she said. "I felt certain he was on a fishing expedition to get me to say more."

A spiral of fear trickled up Cora's spine. After her conversation with Mack this morning, he must have spoken to James and had him inquire about the reasons for them leaving their home.

"What did you tell him?"

Beth bit her lip. "I don't want to lie to James. He's sweet and I like him. He's the best man I've ever had the pleasure of courting. But I also knew I couldn't tell him the truth." She sighed. "I told him we had to leave because I had a suitor that refused to accept it when I told him no. That finally after you threatened to call the sheriff, we decided it was time to leave Charleston behind."

It was partially the truth. She'd only left out where Cora had taken the fireplace poker and knocked a man into his next life. Even now, Cora felt bad that she'd killed a man, but what else could she have done that would have stopped him?

Harrison didn't even pause when she walked into the room and told him to stop.

"That sounds good. I'm sure Mr. Nosy will continue to pursue this line of questioning."

"Cora, there's more you need to know. His wife miscarried at seven months. The baby is buried in the family graveyard. It was after they lost the baby that she took off with the pan peddler. James said they were miserable the last few months they were together. Each one blamed the other for the baby's death."

Stunned, she realized that James was actually telling Beth more than Mack had told her.

"Did he say how the baby died?"

"All he said was that she went into labor when she was only seven months pregnant and the baby didn't survive."

Pain seized Cora's chest at the thought of losing a baby. How did a mother survive? How did a father accept the death of his child? Mack had mentioned that it was not a good time for their marriage. How could it be? Grief did strange things to people and losing a child would be the worst kind of pain.

If they blamed each other for the baby's death, what caused her to go into labor?

That was a question she would need to ask Mack. But would he want to tell her? And what would a woman see in a peddler who traveled the country selling kitchen goods?

There was still so much they needed to discuss and learn about one another and yet, with Mack, she noticed she felt comfortable. At ease.

Unlike any other suitor, she felt safe with Mack.

"Did the two of you have a good time?"

"Oh yes," Beth said with a smile.

"Is that why you came home with your lips all swollen and your hair mussed?"

A giggle came from her sister. "We did do a lot of kissing."

In some ways, Cora felt jealous. Yes, she and Mack had kissed but she wouldn't call it a lot of kissing and her lips had not been swollen or her hair mussed.

"Please be careful, Beth," she said, remembering how she had saved her sister the last time.

"Of course," Beth said. "I didn't think there would be anyone for me here and yet James is perfect."

She lay back on the bed and sighed.

Cora couldn't help but feel slightly jealous. She was supposed to be the one who was making a match and yet Beth and James seemed so far ahead of her and Mack.

"If he asks me to marry him, I will say yes," she said. "Whatever happens between you and Mack is not going to stop me. It's time I found happiness and so should you. If you married Mack, we would be living here right next to one another."

It did seem ideal, but she also knew she wasn't going to promise herself to a man she was uncertain about just to please her sister. Besides, she had this murder hanging over her. Sometimes she wished she would have just gone to the sheriff and taken her chances.

At least then she wouldn't be hiding or slinking around or feeling so guilty that she had killed a man in defense of her sister. But there was no chance the son of a congressman would be punished for trying to ruin a woman.

With a sigh, she glanced at her sister on the bed. "Do you think I should tell Mack about Harrison?"

Beth sat up, shaking her head. "No, you can't. If they find you, they will hang you and it would be all my fault."

"But at least he would know the truth."

"How would you feel if he decided he couldn't marry you because you killed a man? What if he sent you packing? What then?"

It was true, he could tell her to leave because he didn't want a killer in his house.

"Don't ruin my happiness," Beth said quietly. "I want to marry James and if you confess to Mack, then we may both be told to leave."

But how could she not tell Mack? Entering a marriage with secrets was not a good thing and he wouldn't have the chance to decide if he could live with a murderess.

This was something she had not considered. She just thought they would arrive and soon one or both of them would be married. Now she needed to rethink everything because it wasn't fair to Mack or even James not to know the real reason they had left Charleston.

Regardless of what Beth thought, Cora could not keep this secret from Mack. Sooner or later, she would have to tell him. But when?

# CHAPTER 10

*T*he next day, she found another note on the door. This morning's message from Mack had been so sweet, that her heart had pounded in her chest and she stared at the paper, tears welling in her eyes.

*Dearest Cora,*

*Though I never wanted to marry again, I'm so thankful you are in my life. Can't wait to spend the holidays together. Happy Thanksgiving. Let's make today special.*

*Mack*

It was Thanksgiving day and though Montana was not a state and they didn't celebrate the holiday, Mack and James decided for Cora's and Beth's benefits they would have a Thanksgiving feast.

They invited the ranch hands, and today would be a day of giving thanks for what they had. One of Cora's dreams had always been to have a big family and for them all to come together for the holidays. Today, Mack was making her dream come true.

And he seemed like the type of man to make all her dreams come true. They had not kissed since the day he drove her around the ranch and showed her the property, but each morning and each night before they parted ways, he would kiss her on the cheek in front of everyone.

It was a simple gesture, but it felt right and filled her with warmth each time. As much as she had resisted, she was starting to have feelings for Mack. And never before had she ever experienced feelings for any man.

The special way he let her know each morning his feelings about her, the way he kissed her cheek at night, the looks he gave her as they sat across the table from each other, and once he'd even ran his toes up her leg, causing her to blush.

Yes, they were taking it slow, but they each had been hurt before, and right now, they were building trust in each other. That's why it was so important that eventually she tell him the truth about why they left.

It was hard not to compare them to Beth and James who seemed like they were well on their way to marriage. But Mack and Cora were slower and she was grateful he was patient with her.

Though there were still secrets between them. Secrets about his first marriage and her secret of killing someone. Quickly she pushed the awful thought from her mind. Today was Thanksgiving and there would be no thoughts of Harrison and how the law was searching for her.

Dressed in her best dress, she walked out of the bedroom and went into the kitchen to help Hattie.

"Good morning," she said. "Happy Thanksgiving."

"Aw, Cora," she said. "The turkey has been cooking since the wee hours of the morning. The cornbread dressing is in the oven. I'm working on the giblet gravy. Could you please put the homemade rolls in the oven?"

"Of course," Cora said, picking up an apron and wrapping it around her waist.

"I'm so thrilled we're doing this today," Hattie said. "It's a good reminder of how very blessed we are."

Cora did indeed feel very blessed today. This new life she'd chosen might work out after all. Mack had been so attentive in the last week, making certain they had time alone to learn more about each other. And no matter how much she tried to resist him, his gentle caring ways were winning her over. But could he love her when she told him the truth?

As the women worked in the kitchen, Beth was nowhere to be found. She'd not been in bed this morning when Cora crawled out. Obviously, she must be somewhere with James.

"Miss Cora, you and your sister have been so good for this house. I truly hope that soon you and Mack will say your vows. It's been so good to hear laughter echoing through the house."

Why wasn't there laughter before?

"Were the men unhappy before we arrived?"

The woman tsked. "Since his first wife ran off with that hooligan, he's been hurting. He's told you about her, hasn't he?"

Cora so wanted to lie but knew that would break the bond of trust she had with Hattie. "He's told me he's been married before and that they lost a baby."

The woman sighed and shook her head. "I'm so grateful that you're here and hopefully soon there will be children running through this house."

The woman didn't say anything else and Cora didn't press her. "I'll set the table."

Hattie nodded and then began to dish up all the food. There was so much. Between the two of them, Hattie and Cora soon had everything ready.

"I'll call everyone to the table," Cora said.

She walked through the empty house and wondered where everyone was hiding. As she walked outside, she saw the men carrying boxes out of the barn under Beth's direction.

The young girl was going through the boxes, oohing and awing at whatever was inside.

"Time to eat," Cora called.

Beth glanced up at her. "Cora, look, it's Christmas decorations."

A pang squeezed Cora's chest and she realized that since they were here, they could decorate the house for Christmas.

"James said we were welcome to decorate. We can even put up a real tree."

Their parents had never allowed Christmas decorations in the house, and as children, they had hated that time of year. Who didn't allow their children to put up Christmas decorations? Their father. And their mother would never argue with the tyrant.

"Bring them inside the house and we'll look at them after we eat. Tell the hands it's time to wash up."

When everyone was in the house and seated around the table, Cora couldn't help but tear up. She couldn't remember the last time she had sat at a table full of friends and family and enjoyed the holiday.

Mack held out his hand and she took it, thinking he was going to lead a prayer. "Today, we celebrate Thanksgiving. A day of remembering how blessed we are."

He turned and faced Cora. "I didn't want a mail order bride, but my brother insisted. All I can say is I'm so very thankful that you chose me, a grumpy man who'd forgotten the joys of being with a woman. So I'm thankful for you."

Warmth filled her and she smiled. "Thank you. I'm grateful for being here with all of you today. To be living on a ranch in the middle of nowhere, to a house filled with laughter, and for each one of you creating the atmosphere of family, which I've never experienced but longed for very much. And I'm so thankful that Mack, who is not grumpy, put an ad in the gazette."

Sitting beside her, Hattie said what she was grateful for. When it came to Beth, she blushed and turned to James.

"I came here thinking I would be the outsider. That there was no one for me, but then I met James. I'm so grateful that my sister hi...helped me decide to come with her. James, I'm enjoying this time with you and I hope it continues."

Oh, dear, she was going to smack Beth when she got a chance. The silly girl almost said the word *hit*. She almost revealed the real reason they were here. Sooner or later, she was going to let it slip and Cora was growing frightened of how Mack would react.

When everyone had said what they were thankful for, Mack said a blessing over the food and then they begin to eat.

"All the Christmas decorations are in the house. After lunch, let's go through them. Maybe this weekend we can pick out a Christmas tree," Beth said, her voice raised with excitement.

It had been so long since they had a truly great Christmas, but if Beth didn't stop almost slipping, Cora would find herself celebrating in jail. And maybe that's what she deserved.

"You're not eating very much," Mack said as he leaned closer to her.

She loved the way he smelled. It was a mixture of man, outdoors, and leather, and every time he got close, she inhaled deeply.

What could she say? Her appetite seemed to have suddenly waned after her sister almost revealed their secret. Sooner or later, Beth would tell them all. The woman could not keep a secret to save her life. Only this time, it was Cora's life.

"My mind drifted back to past holidays with my mother and father," she said. But what she didn't tell him was that they started out good and by the end of the day, her mother would lock herself in her bedroom while their drunken father was hell to live with. Everyone made themselves scarce, so he could rant and rave and destroy all on his own.

"Come back to me," Mack said as he leaned in close. "I thought we could go for a ride together this afternoon. We won't have many more warm days and it would be nice to spend some time alone."

"That would be lovely," she said, thinking maybe it was time to tell him the truth. Maybe he needed to know how she had killed Harrison.

"If you guys are thinking about using the buggy, I've already got it hitched and ready to go," James said. "I'm taking Beth out looking for a Christmas tree."

"That's a job for all of us," Mack said.

"Not me," Hattie replied. "I'm planning on sitting in my room and reading. You boys like that cold weather. Not me."

Mack gazed at Cora. "Do you want to cut a Christmas tree?"

A bubble of excitement filled her and she smiled. "I would love to."

"Great," Mack said. "We're going to find a Christmas tree, and this time, James will drive the wagon, and Cora and I will sit in the back."

A grin spread across her face and she couldn't wait to spend the afternoon with Mack.

# CHAPTER 11

*M*ack decided that after today, they would celebrate every Thanksgiving, whether Montana did or not. It was such a great day to give thanks and to spend time with the women he felt would soon be their wives.

All that was holding him back from asking was the secret that had eaten at him like an illness since Margery lost the baby. How could he tell Cora that he feared it was his fault his wife miscarried? That because he upset his wife and made her cry, she had gone into early labor.

That his son died because of him.

No, he wasn't a great husband, or at least, he hadn't been to Margery. So why would he even consider marrying Cora?

"You're frowning," she said, gazing up at him.

"I'm just remembering the past and having doubts

about what I'm doing," he said, knowing that probably wasn't a great thing to say, but it was true.

"Doubts about the two of us?"

"Yes," he said. "Why would you want a man whose first wife left him for another man? Who caused the death of his own child."

They had been walking through the forest, James and Beth ahead of them. She stopped and pulled him to a halt. "Explain yourself."

With a sigh, he pulled off his cowboy hat and ran his hand through his hair. "I never meant to hurt Margery. She was seven months pregnant and she wanted me to drive her into town to get more yarn for a baby blanket she was making."

He paused his mind going back to that awful day.

"The clouds were building outside and I knew that meant a storm was coming in. I needed to make certain the animals had plenty of feed, water, and food to last them for several days. Plus, I didn't want to get into town and be stuck there."

Reaching down, he picked up a stick and took out his carving knife. He began to whittle it down. His hands shook as he ran the knife down the wood.

"That's understandable, but why do you think that's what caused her to miscarry?"

Lifting his gaze to hers, he remembered the terrible tantrum she'd thrown. "Because she cried so hard, she made herself sick. She threw things, she screamed at me. Once she even tried to hit me. All because I wouldn't risk my life, hers, and the baby's by going into town to buy more yarn. And I wasn't about to let her go by herself."

Cora shook her head. "I'm sorry that happened to you and to her, but you were being the more logical person. You were thinking of her and even the animals. What if you'd taken her to town, and halfway there, a blizzard had struck? All three of you would have died."

It was true, but still, there were so many times he wished he'd just said yes and loaded her up in the wagon and taken her into town with him. Maybe then they would all still be alive.

"Did a storm hit?"

"Yes," he said. "It was blowing so hard, we would never have made it into town and yet she blamed me until her water broke and she went into labor." He went back to furiously whittling on the stick and she watched him carve it into an arrow. "There was no way to reach a doctor. I had to deliver our son."

Tears welled in Mack's eyes. "The baby was so tiny. He opened his eyes, looked at me, and then he died in my arms. He needed another two months in his mother's womb."

Cora reached out and placed her hand on his arm and squeezed. "I can't imagine the pain of holding your baby while it died. What about Margery? How did she do?"

The memory of her calling him all kinds of names made him jerk. "She blamed me for the baby's death. It was all my fault. If I had done what she wanted, then he would still be alive. Three months after his death, she ran off with the pan peddler, leaving me to cope with my grief alone."

Though the storm had dropped two feet of fresh snow. They would never have made it into town.

When she left, she'd crushed his heart. How could she leave him after the death of their son? How?

"You know that's not true," Cora said. "If you had taken her out in the storm and she'd gone into labor all of you would be dead."

She stepped into his arms and he wrapped his arms around Cora. Why did this feel right? Why did she seem like a reasonable woman? Why did he get a sense of homecoming with her in his arms?

"While I know that's true, it's hard not to believe what she said. I wanted that boy. I wanted my marriage to work. And for that reason, I'm afraid. What if after we marry, you decide I'm the worst man you've ever experienced and I'm not worthy of you?"

He lived in fear of waking up one day to the same kind of marriage he'd had before.

"What if you decide I'm the worst woman and you can do better? I have just as many fears about marriage as you do. You've experienced it once, all I've ever seen about love and marriage is from my parents, and believe me, that is not something I would never want."

He grabbed her hand and brought it up to his lips. "Do you think it's my fault that our son died?"

Why was he pushing her? He didn't know, but for years he'd carried this guilt, this burden of killing his only child and he didn't want to feel that any longer. He'd loved that child the moment they knew they were going to have it.

"God took your son home to be an angel. There wasn't a thing you could have done to have prevented him from dying. Who knows what caused Margery's water to break, but you were there by her side, you delivered your baby and then you held him while he slipped away to heaven. Don't blame yourself. Don't blame Margery. It was God's will."

Tears welled in his eyes and he stared at Cora. For years, he'd blamed himself, and yet, what she said made sense.

Pulling her into his arms, he held onto her so tightly that he feared he was crushing her. No, he had not wanted Cora, but she was the best thing that had ever happened to him.

Leaning back, he tilted her chin up until his lips could claim hers. He kissed her until all he wanted to do was lay her down in the snow and take her right there, but that could never happen.

Finally, they broke apart. She gazed up into his eyes and he could see the confusion there. "You, Mack Lawson, are not a grumpy man, but rather a sad man whose life has dealt a lot of tragedy."

"And you, Cora Weaver, have made me feel so much better," he said, releasing her and taking her hand. "We better find Beth and James and that Christmas tree. If I'm alone with you much longer, you're not going to be safe from me."

Reaching up, she ran her hand down his cheek. "Thank you for telling me about your son. I know that could not have been easy for you."

He touched his lips to hers and then they began to walk toward the wagon. "Cora, you're a fine woman."

"Thank you," she said.

"Someday, you're going to tell me your secrets. Someday soon."

# CHAPTER 12

*A* week later, the house was decorated for Christmas. The pine tree had been chopped down and now sat in the house with the decorations from their past Christmases.

James and Mack were out in the barn, grooming the horses and talking.

"Have you gotten Cora anything for Christmas yet?" James asked.

"No, I'm still trying to decide what to get her," he said, uncertain. They were growing closer, but she had yet to reveal her secret and he knew she had one.

There were times she was nervous as a kitten, especially when someone new came to the ranch. Just last week, one of the neighbors dropped by and she'd hidden in the house, quivering. What was wrong with her?

"I'm going to ask Beth to marry me before Christmas. I was thinking of a Christmas Eve wedding. It would be nice if we could make it a double wedding."

Mack looked up from the horse he was currying and stared at his brother. "Are you certain about this? Don't forget this marriage business is hard. Remember how in love me and Margery were and then we got married. It's not easy."

James gave a little laugh. "Do you remember the way Mom and Papa use to be around each other? How happy they were? I remember catching them kissing in the kitchen and Papa had his hand on Mom's behind and she wasn't telling him no."

Their parents had the best marriage, and yes, he remembered how happy they were. Sure, they would have disagreements, but often they ended with them laughing at the other one. Everything worked without them throwing things at one another or cursing or yelling and screaming. The only time he remembered his mother screaming was when one of them was in danger or if they disobeyed. Then she would shout and scream the rafters down trying to protect them.

One winter, Mother came down with pneumonia and she never recovered. Papa was lost without her and he died three years later.

"I think you should ask Cora to marry you," James said.

"Not yet. I'm not ready and I don't think she is either. Something is bothering her and she has yet to tell me. Something I think happened back in Charleston."

James stopped what he was doing and stared at Mack. "And you want me to pressure Beth into telling me. That wouldn't be right."

Maybe not, but Mack wanted her to tell him.

"You're right, it wouldn't be. I keep waiting for her to tell me, but she's taking her sweet time."

"What do you think it is? A broken engagement? A man took advantage of her? They robbed a bank? What?"

They did seem to have plenty of money. Cora had been removing cash from the hems of her dresses and he was shocked to see how much cash she had. What if they had robbed a bank? What would he do then?

"I'm not really wanting to marry a woman who would have the law looking for her. I can't imagine having to tell our children that she's in prison or she was hung."

Laughter seemed to explode from James. "Come on. I don't think that our girls could have robbed a bank. It has to be something to do with a broken engagement."

Mack certainly hoped that was her secret, but it had to be something worse.

"Why wouldn't she have already told me. She told me about one man cheating on her. This one has her uneasy."

They continued to work, each man pondering what Cora's secret was. When they finished, they gave the animals fresh hay in their stalls, feed and water, and then stood around.

"Do you have feelings for Cora?"

He sighed. "I care about her. I enjoy her company, and there are days I believe I'm falling in love with her, but then just like yesterday when Mr. Jenkins stopped by, she got all nervous and stayed in the house. What about you? The two of you are almost running to the preacher."

James grinned. "The sooner the better. I've bought her a ring and I'm just waiting for the right time to ask her to marry me. I think she'll say yes."

Mack felt a little jealous. He remembered that excitement the first time he married. The anxiousness of whether she would say yes or if her father would agree to their marriage.

It had been an exciting time and he needed not to bring his brother down. Hopefully his marriage would last and be only once. Unlike Mack who now knew the dangers.

"If Beth is who you want to marry and you love her, then I wish you nothing but happiness. If you think she'll stand by your side, through the good times and the bad, then you need to put a ring on her finger. You must do what makes you and Beth happy. Don't worry about me and Cora. We will either catch up and want to say I do, or somewhere along the way, she'll return to Charleston."

And Mack knew he didn't want her returning to Charleston. He just wasn't certain of what he wanted.

"Thanks, brother. Of course, I'd like for you to stand beside me when I marry Beth."

"Of course," Mack said. "Who knows? It could still be a double wedding. I just need to understand more about what is bothering Cora. It's not good to go into a marriage with secrets between you. She knows mine and now I must learn hers."

"Does she know about how Margery ran off and left you?"

Mack thought for a moment. "Yes, I told her. You know I just want the time we spend together to be happy. I like the way she smiles. And when she touches me, I'm not immune. My heart beats faster and my mind starts going in directions that it has no business thinking about."

James started laughing. "I don't think you're immune from Cora. I think you just haven't recognized that you're in love with her."

"Maybe so, but I need answers before I can promise her forever."

# CHAPTER 13

*A* week later, Beth and Cora were getting ready for bed. Tonight they had played games until their eyes were drooping.

"Tonight was fun," Beth said as she slipped her nightgown on over her head.

"Yes, it was," Cora admitted as she sat in front of the mirror on the dresser, brushing her long hair.

A shiver rippled through her. "It's such a cold night."

"That's why we all need to get married. Just think, we could be snuggled in bed with our husbands to keep us warm."

That thought was both intriguing and terrifying. Cora knew only the basics of what went on between a man and a woman in the marital bed. What if she didn't like it?

"True, but we've both seen what a bad marriage is like. Is that what you want?"

"No, James and I have talked about what we expect and I don't think for a minute he would put up with me if I acted like our father."

"What if he acts like father?"

That was Cora's biggest fear. What if after they married, her husband became like her father, drinking too much, screaming, yelling, and destroying furniture. She couldn't live like that again.

"No, he wouldn't do that. He talks about his parents' marriage and says that's what he wants. All I know is that I want my marriage not to be like Mama and Papa's. My children will never be a witness to something like theirs. I'll die an old maid before that happens."

Cora crawled in. "And you're certain about James? That he will give you the marriage you want?"

"More than any man I've ever met."

A sigh escaped Cora. She was happy for her sister, she really was, but she was also concerned. What if James was like Harrison? What if he...

"Don't even start comparing him to Harrison," Beth whispered as she blew out the lantern and crawled into bed.

"You thought you were in love with him," Cora said.

"Not really. I wanted to be in love so badly, to find a man and settle down, but I didn't know what to look for in a man. And living there, we certainly attracted enough bad men. It seemed like everyone you and I courted were slimy."

It was true. All they seemed to attract were the carpetbaggers and thieves.

"Maybe that's all that were available at the time," Cora said, remembering the men of Charleston. The good men seemed to all be taken and the ones left over were not worth marrying.

Just then the howl of a coyote not too far from the house echoed through the house.

A shiver rippled through her. "I don't like that sound. It's eerie and haunting."

"They can't get in the house," Beth said. "We're safe. And Mack and James wouldn't let them hurt us."

They wouldn't. She knew that, but the sound was so lonely sounding. It was like the animal knew how the inside of her soul was and he echoed her feelings.

"I hope he finds a female coyote soon," Cora said.

Beth giggled. "Thank you, sister, for making me come with you to Montana. I never would have imagined I would find a husband here."

"You're more likely to get married than me," Cora said, knowing it was true.

For a moment, she was quiet as she settled in beneath the covers. "You and Mack are both being so cautious. You're both so afraid of getting hurt again that you won't take a chance on one another. He's a good man. Give him a chance."

Was it true? Yes, she was being cautious. But there was more to it than that.

"Are you going to tell James the reason why we came to Angel Creek?"

Beth lay there and Cora could almost feel her brain churning. Finally she spoke, "Yes, but not until you tell Mack. They deserve to know before we marry them."

Thank God she was seeing reason. Cora had been holding back, waiting for Beth to come to this realization. And now finally she had.

"Yes," Cora said. "I've been thinking I should tell him soon, but then I get nervous. The next time we're alone, I'll tell him. He knows. How do you think he figured it out?"

Laughter came from Beth's side of the bed. "Hmm, just because you're jumpier than a kitten. Always looking over your shoulder, expecting the sheriff from Charleston to arrive any minute."

It was true. She worried all the time about the law finding her and yet she couldn't tell anyone about her fears.

"If I could do anything to take back that night, I would. I didn't want to kill him."

"I know. And if only I had listened to you and realized he was only after our inheritance. That's all he wanted. Not my love."

At least her sister seemed to have learned something from the experience. What had Cora learned? That a good person could not forgive herself when she did something wrong. Even if she hadn't meant to harm the man. He'd been trying to molest her sister and she couldn't let him get away with it.

"What do you think Papa would have done if he were alive?" Beth asked.

Beth always wanted her parents to become decent people. She wanted her father to protect them, fight for them, and not keel over drunk.

"You don't want to hear my answer," Cora said. "You know how I feel about Papa's drinking and Momma's hiding from the destruction he was causing. Only what she didn't realize was that we were affected by her cowardice. She didn't protect us from Papa."

"True," Beth said softly. "You are now an avenging angel determined to protect us. And I've become the person who needs validation. Love. Someone to make me feel like a decent human being again."

"Oh, Beth, you are a decent person. It's just that we've been through so much. Coming here to Angel Creek was the best decision we've ever made."

"Yes," Beth said. "I'm so glad you convinced me to come along. Otherwise, I would have remained in that hellhole waiting for a decent man."

They lay in the darkness and again the coyote howled his lonesome song of heartache and pain. While both girls had suffered through their childhood of their father's drinking, for the first time in years, Cora felt at peace being in a place where the city would not enjoy seeing her hang.

"Cora, promise me that if something ever happens to

me, that if I have children, you'll take good care of them. I trust you to make certain they have a good life."

"Of course, now go to sleep. Nothing is going to happen to you."

Lying there, all Cora could think about was Harrison. How had his mother felt when she learned of her son's death? With a sigh, she rolled over. Why did he have to die that night?

Because if he had not died, then she would not have been in Angel Creek, Montana.

# CHAPTER 14

*C*ora tossed and turned until she knew she might as well get up. After talking to Beth, she'd come to the realization that she must tell Mack the truth before they went any further. He needed to know she had killed a man.

And yet, she liked the place they were finally in. It seemed like in the last few days they had started to accept and like the other person. They were starting to trust one another and she knew this would destroy what they had built together.

And she wasn't ready for that to end.

What she needed was a warm cup of tea to settle her tangled nerves and let her rest. Putting her wrapper on and her slippers, she slipped out of the bedroom and to the kitchen.

When she entered the room, a dark shadow moved and she stifled a scream.

SYLVIA MCDANIEL

"Cora?" Mack asked.

"Yes," she whispered.

"Easy, it's just me."

Her breath released in a whoosh as she came into the kitchen.

"What are you doing up?"

"I can't sleep. I was going to make some tea. Would you like a cup?"

"Yes, please. I was checking on Ebony, our mare. Her time is near and I thought she might have been going into labor this afternoon. But she's fine."

Cora pumped water out of the pump and into the kettle. "Did you hear the coyotes?"

"Yes," Mack said. "It's a full moon and they're courting the females."

She sighed and glanced out the window before she placed the kettle on the fire. "It's so bright outside with the moon reflecting on the snow."

"Yes," he said. "Not a good night for rabbits or small prey to be roaming. The hawks and owls will scoop them right up."

Taking two cups down, she put the tea in a tea ball and put it inside his cup. When the tea whistle began to blow, she quickly picked up the container and poured the hot liquid over the tea ball. Once she was finished with his, she did one for her.

"Why couldn't you sleep?" he asked.

How much should she tell him? How had she

90

reached the conclusion she needed to tell him she was a murderess?

"Beth and I were talking about marriage before she fell asleep. How neither one of us wants a marriage like our parents had. We talked for a while and, of course, James and even you came into the conversation."

"What kind of marriage do you want?"

"One like your parents," she said softly. "I've seen the worst of marriage, now I'd like to experience a good one. You've lived the worst of marriage. What do you want?"

"I want one like my parents as well. Life is too short to be fighting and arguing, and I want a happy life."

The wood popped in the woodstove creating sparks of light in the darkened kitchen.

"Bad things are bound to happen," Cora said. "It's life."

"Yes, but if we stand strong together and support each other, then we could have a happy life."

Cora smiled in the darkness at Mack.

"Beth thinks James is going to ask her to marry him any day now," she said softly.

Mack grinned. "He's been talking to me about whether or not to ask her. What do you think?"

Tears welled in Cora's eyes. She wanted her sister to be happy and James seemed like he would care for her.

"As long as your brother loves and takes care of my sister, I'll be so happy for them. Beth experienced a bad marriage growing up, so she knows what she wants in life. All I ask is that he make her happy."

Mack reached across the table and took her hand in his. "That's all we can hope for."

"Yes," she said, wiping a tear from her eye.

"Aw, honey, don't cry, this should be a happy time," he said standing.

"These are happy tears," she said though part of her was sad. Sad that soon she would have to tell Mack about what happened and she didn't want anything to change between them. She wanted them to continue to be happy.

Pulling her up to standing, he took her in his arms and held her tightly against him. She loved the feel of his strong chest, the way he smelled of man and leather, the way he sheltered her in his arms, and knew this would be what it was like in a storm.

"Come on, honey, we need to go to bed," he said and took her gently by the arm.

At the doorway into the living area and to his bedroom, he glanced up. "Look?"

"What?"

He pointed up at the top of the doorway. "Mistletoe."

A grin spread across his face and he pulled her into his arms.

"You're going to kiss me," she said in a whispered voice.

"It's bad luck if I don't kiss you," he said. "And we want the very best luck."

"Yes," she said as his lips came down to hers.

This wasn't a gentle kiss, but the kiss of a man who wanted her. And she could feel the hard edges of his body that let her know just exactly how much he wanted her. His mouth claimed hers and he kissed her like he was going to brand his lips on hers. Seal them together in a way that would promise them forever.

Finally, when she felt faint, she pushed against his chest. "Mack."

"Yes, darling," he said. "I wanted to give you a kiss to dream about tonight. Just like I'm going to be dreaming about you."

The thought sent spirals of warmth flooding through her body straight to her center.

"Goodnight, sweet Cora," he said as he released her and turned to his bedroom. She watched him walk away and the urge to follow him was strong as she raised her hand to her lips, and her other hand, she placed on her heart.

The heart she had managed to lose to Mack Lawson. It was time to tell him the truth, and if he still wanted her after he learned she had killed a man, then she would marry him.

But first, she had to tell him the truth.

# CHAPTER 15

The night of meeting with Cora in the kitchen had stayed with Mack. All he could think about was if they were married, they would have returned to bed together. The way she looked in her robe, her hair flowing down her back, the way she teared up when they spoke about Beth and James marrying.

This woman was different than Margery. But then, Mack was different as well. He was more certain of what he expected in a marriage and he wasn't going to settle for anything less than what he wanted.

Christmas would soon be arriving. So he'd snuck off to town to do some shopping and also to look about getting Cora a wedding ring. It didn't mean he was certain of marrying her. It didn't mean he wasn't uncertain either. But this way, he would have the ring if he made the decision she was what he wanted.

As he walked through the streets of Angel Creek, he couldn't help but notice the small town was growing. He went into the mercantile, and as he strolled around, he found a book of poems by William Blake for Cora. She loved to read and she would enjoy the beautiful sonnets. He also picked up a new apron for Hattie, a hat for Beth, and for his brother a flannel shirt.

It was a joke that every year, they purchased each other a new flannel shirt to replace the old one they had worn out.

With all his purchases wrapped, he saved the best for last.

"What kind of wedding rings do you have?" he asked Cassie Weston, the owner of the mercantile.

The woman pulled out a box filled with gold bands and even some with a small diamond on them.

"You getting married again?" she asked.

This was why he had not wanted to look at rings because it would get around town that Mack Lawson remarrying.

"Not yet," he said. "I'm going to buy a ring and then if I get the notion to get married, I'll be ready."

"Oh," the woman said. "I thought maybe that pretty lady you picked up at the stagecoach depot, you were going to marry her."

"We're talking," he said. "I'm not ready to ask her yet, but we're talking."

The woman smiled.

"This band is so pretty. It has just a small row of diamonds on the gold band."

"How much is that one?"

She gave him the price and he looked it over. It was fancier than the ring he'd bought Margery, but that was good. Cora deserved something so much better if he decided to marry her.

"I'll take it," he said.

The woman wrapped it up.

"Good luck, Mack. You deserve happiness," she told him.

"Thank you."

Quickly he walked out of the store, climbed on his horse, and began the long trek home.

What was he doing? He'd promised himself he would never marry again. That he would never give his heart to a woman again, and yet just the thought of Cora had him spurring his horse, anxious to get home to her.

He promised himself he would never do this again, but somehow in the last month, Cora had won his heart. Even with a grumpy ad, she'd overcome his objections and agreed with him that there was no reason to hurry. She seemed to love living on the ranch and was learning more and more about the life of a ranch wife.

Somehow during the last month, he'd fallen in love with Cora and now all he wanted to do was make her his in every sense of the word. He wanted to stand before a preacher and say their vows and then he wanted to claim her as his wife.

To make her love him as much as he'd fallen in love with her.

Whatever her secret was that she had yet to confess to, they would deal with it together. Nothing was going to come between them. This time, he felt certain about marrying. About giving Cora his heart. About the two of them being happy together.

With that, he spurred his horse and headed home. He had to see her. The ring in his pocket was like a heavy stone connected to his heart. Soon, he would ask her to marry him. When the time was right.

# CHAPTER 16

*T*oday's message from Mack read...

*Dearest Cora,*

*Every morning your smile makes me warm. Your laughter fills my heart and your kiss makes me long for you. Christmas will soon be here and I can't wait to spend our first Christmas together.*

*Mack*

The man wrote the sweetest messages and she'd grown accustomed to waking and reading them each morning. They made her heart beat faster and put a smile on her face. How could anyone not be happy being married to this man and yet she was still afraid. Soon, she had to tell him the truth. Soon.

Last night, they agreed to go into town for shopping. It was only twelve days before Christmas and she needed to buy gifts for everyone.

As soon as she was ready, she walked out to find Mack waiting for her.

"Your sleigh awaits," he said.

"Sleigh?"

"Yes, after that last snow, we'll now be traveling by sleigh."

"How exciting," she said, thinking she'd never been in a sleigh before. "And we'll fill it with packages just like Santa."

A grin spread across his face. "Let's go."

On the way into town, she sat next to him and thought back about that first day when he'd picked up her and Beth from the stage depot. She'd been so nervous, so afraid, and so fearful that he would expect marriage that very first day.

"Tell me more about Angel Creek," she said. "That first day, I don't know if I saw anything."

He grinned at her and pulled her in closer. The sun was out, but a cold wind blew, and it was cold even with the two of them sitting so close together.

"Remind me to look for a coat for you and some boots while we're there," he said. "We need to get Beth some as well."

She didn't want him to feel like he had to buy her things; she and Beth had money. "I can pay for it."

With a big frown on his face, he turned to her. "No, I pay for everything. Your money is yours."

While she appreciated him saying this, she didn't want to be dependent on him. The only thing her father had done right in his life was leave them an inheritance, which she was thankful for.

"Not my Christmas presents," she said.

A laugh rippled up from his chest. "Miss Weaver, are you arguing with me?"

"No, I'm telling you how it's going to be. I will pay for my Christmas presents," she said. "If you want to pay for my coat and boots, I will allow it, only if you consider it part of my Christmas."

A grin spread across his face and he reached down and kissed her. "If this is how we fight, I think I can say, not bad."

Warmth spread through Cora as she remembered her parents fighting about everything, her father calling her mother a stupid bitch, and her mother throwing a plate at her father in response.

"As long as we're equal partners, honey, we'll get along just great," she said in a soft whisper. On the way back, she planned on telling him about the murder. She wanted to confess to him and then if he didn't want her, she had decided she would turn herself in.

Living with this horror of what she'd done was eating her alive and she needed to confess to someone. Even after she told him, she wanted to tell the law in Angel Creek. Hopefully, the sheriff would hear her out and help her.

Unlike what would have happened in Charleston. There she had no chance, but here the law might listen to reason.

When they arrived at the mercantile, they entered the store and the clerk called out. "Hello, Mack. Who is this pretty woman?"

"This is Cora," he said. "We'd like to do some shopping."

"Hi, Cora, I'm Cassie Weston, my husband and I own the mercantile."

"Nice to meet you," Cora replied.

"Let me know if you have any questions," she said.

They separated in the store, each going a different direction. Quickly, she found a necklace for Beth, a knife for James, and a small bottle of lavender-scented perfume for Hattie.

She carried her purchases to the counter and it was then she spotted the pocket watch—silver with a horse reared up on his hind legs. She glanced around the store and didn't see Mack.

"May I see that watch," she asked.

"Of course," she said. "And I'll keep an eye out for Mack."

Cora held the timepiece in her hand and when she opened it, tears sprang to her eyes. Engraved inside was an inscription. *Time started with you.*

The words were perfect and seemed to fit the two of them, saying what her heart was telling her.

She snapped it shut, blinking rapidly to keep anyone from seeing her tears.

"I'll take it," she said. "Can you wrap it quickly so he doesn't see it?"

"Of course," the woman said with a smile. "Mack's a good man. You couldn't do any better. I'm so happy for him and for you."

Cora blushed. "Thank you."

A few minutes later, he came to the counter. "Try these boots on."

"All right," she said. Sinking down into a nearby chair, she slipped her feet into the boots. They fit her perfectly.

"I need two pairs of those boots," he said.

Next, he had her try on the coat and the first one was too large, but the next one fit, and they added that to the stack.

By now, she was starving.

"Let's grab a bite to eat at the cafe while she packs this all up for us," Cora said.

"Great idea," he said. "Only if I can pay."

She laughed. "Not if I get the check first."

He pulled her close and they walked down the street toward the cafe.

As they rounded the corner, her heart plummeted to her feet. She gasped. Stopping on the wooden sidewalk, trying to get her lungs to expand, she stared at the apparition walking down the street. She stood next to Mack, stiff as she watched Harrison.

How had he found her? How? He was dead.

"No," she cried. "No, it can't be."

Mack grabbed Cora by the arms. "What's wrong? Are you all right?"

With horror, she watched as Harrison strolled toward the saloon. She didn't know if he'd seen her or not, but he must know she was here. But he was dead. There had been no pulse. No breath. No heartbeat.

Had she just seen a ghost?

"Come on, honey, I'm taking you inside the cafe. Then you're going to explain to me what happened."

With a sigh, she knew it was past time. Today she would tell him everything.

# CHAPTER 17

*A*fter they sat at a table, Mack ordered Cora a cup of hot tea and himself a coffee. When the waitress brought them menus, Cora wouldn't even look.

"I'm not hungry."

"A minute ago you were starving," he said.

"That was before I saw a ghost," she said, shaking her head. "I don't even believe in ghosts."

"Good, me neither," he said. "Tell me what happened back there."

Her face was white and her eyes had grown as large as fifty-cent pieces. She'd been truly frightened.

For the next ten minutes, she told him about how this man Harrison was courting Beth. The son of a congressman and a very eligible suitor. Until the night he attacked Beth and intended to ruin her.

"When I came downstairs, I screamed at him to stop, but he ignored me. Finally, I picked up the fireplace poker and I smacked him on the back. It did nothing. So then I hit him on the head and he collapsed. Beth pushed him off and he fell to the floor. At first, I thought he had just passed out, but then when I saw the blood, I became concerned."

She took a deep breath and shook her head. "I checked his breathing. Nothing. I laid my hand on his chest to feel his heart. Nothing. I tried to shake him awake. Nothing. At that point, I assumed I had killed him."

Placing her face in her hands, she cried. "I didn't want to kill him. I didn't want to murder another human being. And yet there he was on the floor not moving or breathing. We thought he was dead."

"What did you do?"

"I wanted to contact the sheriff, but Beth told me no. They would hang me. He was the son of a congressman. We were two girls who lived alone, whose father had a horrible reputation for causing trouble."

She glanced into his eyes, hers filled with tears. "I had been reading the *Mail Order Bride Gazette* all evening for fun. Yes, I knew we needed to get out of Charleston, but I had no idea how and that magazine had given me some ideas. Beth and I looked through the gazette and decided on your ad because you were so far away and I liked the way you admitted you were grumpy."

That all seemed so long ago now.

"Is this your secret?"

"Yes," she said. "Today I had decided I was going to

tell you on the way home. If you decided you didn't want anything to do with me, I was going to turn myself into the law. Even now, I should probably talk to the sheriff. But he's alive. I know that was him. And he's here. He's coming after me and Beth. I just know it."

Mack reached out and took her hand in his.

"He'll have to come through me and James to get to you girls. He's not going to win. I don't give a damn if he is a congressman's son."

Mack was ready to find him and take care of this right now.

"Let's go find him," he said.

"No, Mack. Not without James. I don't trust him and I fear he'll do something crooked and I couldn't stand the thought of losing you because of him."

His other hand covered hers.

"You're not going to lose me," he said.

"All these months I worried I had killed a man and he's not even dead."

"No one would've blamed you if you had."

"I've been so afraid I'd be arrested and hung for murder. I guess I didn't kill him after all. What do we do now?"

Mack wanted to go after the man, to find him and make certain this man was on his way out of town, but knew that Cora would not allow him to leave her. She was terrified.

"We go home and I protect you. If this Harrison even

attempts to bring charges against you, we'll make certain the truth comes out."

Cora gave him a grateful smile. "You're too good to me, Mack."

"I'd like to be better to you. Cora, marry me. Let me protect you."

A sad smile crossed her face. "That's not a reason to marry, Mack. We both know that."

Mack wanted to kick himself. Why in the hell was he so scared to tell her how he felt about her. Why couldn't he tell her that he loved her and this was just an excuse to make her his. Or even better, why didn't he get down on bended knee and ask her.

But now, she was not going to say yes because she didn't believe he was asking for the right reasons. Not until his heart was full of love for her.

"Let's go home," he said as he rose from the table and threw down some coins to pay for their tea.

Harrison had ruined their day and Mack had the worst timing. Now he needed to get her home and prepare the ranch to keep her safe.

# CHAPTER 18

As soon as they arrived at the ranch, Cora motioned for Beth and the two of them disappeared into the bedroom.

"Harrison is not dead," she said, sinking down onto the bed.

"What? No, he was dead when we left him," Beth said.

"I just saw him in town. Mack noticed how I suddenly grew tense and became so afraid of him seeing me. Mack knows everything. He wanted to go after Harrison, but I talked him out of it. I was so afraid that Harrison would hurt Mack. I love him. I can't lose him."

Her sister smiled. "I'm so happy to hear you say that. James proposed this afternoon while you two were gone. We're planning on a Christmas Eve wedding in town at the church. You know, sister, I would love for you to join us. A double-ring ceremony."

Tears welled in Cora's eyes and she hugged her sister. "I'm so happy for you. But until this situation with Harrison is resolved, I can't marry anyone."

Cora was terrified that the law would believe him and not her. Why didn't they check the body to see if it was cold? Because she'd never killed anyone before.

And she never would.

"I'm so happy for you and James. He'll make you an excellent husband," Cora said, crying softly, remembering Mack's proposal. But that was not the correct reason for marrying.

"And Mack would make you one as well," Beth said. "And if you love him, why are you saying no?"

"Because when he asked me today, he said he wanted to protect me. He didn't say he loved me and that's what I need to hear. I can get protection from any man, but I can't get love. And I need a marriage that is filled with love."

In the last month, she had started to believe in love and now she needed to hear those words before she would agree to marry.

Beth nodded. "James told me he loves me."

"Oh, I'm so happy for you."

"What are we going to do about Harrison?"

Suddenly there was a knock on the door. "Beth and Cora, we need to talk."

Oh no, they were going to tell them to leave. They had attempted to kill a man and suddenly the men didn't want anything to do with them. She'd just ruined Beth's happiness.

Her chest ached with sorrow as she slowly stood from the bed.

"I'm sorry, Beth," Cora said, tears falling from her eyes.

"For what?"

"I'm afraid they're going to tell us to leave," she said.

"Oh come on, they're men and they love us, even if Mack hasn't realized it yet."

After Cora wiped her eyes, they walked out the door and met the men in the living area.

"I've told James about this Harrison character. We need to watch the ranch a little more carefully," Mack said.

James frowned. "Beth and Cora, I don't want you riding alone. No trips by yourselves until we learn what this man wants."

Stunned, Cora stared at them, her mouth gaping. "You're not going to ask us to leave?" Cora asked.

Both men glanced at one another in shock. "No. Why would we?"

"I thought that since I tried to kill a man, you would want us to go."

"You did it protecting your sister, the woman I love," James said. "Frankly, I only wish you'd finished the deed."

Astounded, she listened as they supported her and the reason she had tried to kill him.

Mack shook his head. "No, darling, we don't want you to leave. In fact, I think maybe some shooting lessons are in order so you know how to shoot him next time."

Beth giggled. "Told you."

"We just need to be extra cautious until we learn what he wants. He came here for either revenge or to take you back to Charleston and neither is happening," Mack said.

Cora stared at the people she loved. This was her family and now if only Mack would tell her he loved her, she would marry him in a heartbeat. These were the people she would die protecting.

Out of something bad, she now had the family she'd always wanted. She had a shining example of love.

"Thank you," she said softly. "Thank you for protecting us."

She glanced at Mack, the urge to say she loved him on the tip of her tongue. This afternoon, maybe she should have said yes. But she wanted him to say he loved her before she could agree to become his wife. She needed those three words because never before had she heard them. Not even from her parents.

# CHAPTER 19

*C*hristmas was only days away, and so far, they had not seen any signs of Harrison. Mack and James had alerted the ranch hands and everyone was keeping an eye out for him.

This morning, it was Cora's turn to gather the eggs and she wrapped up in her new coat and wore the boots Mack had purchased for her. Today, she wanted to make cookies for the ranch hands as a Christmas gift. It was hard being so far from town and yet she wanted them to receive some kind of package to open when they celebrated the holiday.

She thought of the message on her door this morning from Mack.

*Dearest Cora,*

*You are the brightest star in my universe. You make me smile, you make me laugh and this Christmas will be filled with joy because of you.*

*Mack*

Why had he not told her he loved her? Why had he not asked her to marry him again, saying the words she longed to hear? With a sigh, she went to do her daily chore.

As she walked outside, the air was crisp with the sun not above the horizon yet. She loved Mack and if he would only say that he loved her as well, she would agree to be his wife.

The thought of her children being raised here on the ranch made her happy. It was so much cleaner than Charleston and here they would learn to be self-sufficient. But before there could be children, there must be a marriage and that would never happen if Mack didn't love her.

With a sigh, she went into the enclosed chicken pen and collected the eggs. The hens had come to accept her and the one hen no longer pecked her. Today, she collected half a dozen eggs before she walked out into the dark morning, closing the door behind her.

A gun poked into her back. "Don't say a word or you're a dead woman."

Harrison. How had gotten onto the ranch property without someone detecting him?

Grabbing her arm, he pulled her away from the chicken pen. She dropped the basket of eggs, so the men would know that something happened to her.

The smelly man kicked it up under some bushes. "No

need for anyone to know that you've been taken," he said with a laugh.

They walked into the pine trees and she knew she had to scream now or he would win. If he was going to kill her, she would rather die here than be on the road with him for months.

She opened her mouth to scream and he put the gun in her face. "Go ahead. It will give me great pleasure to kill you."

With a gun in her face, it was hard to scream.

"Now get on my horse."

"It's winter. You can't take me back to Charleston now," she said. "We'll die of the cold."

He cocked his gun. "Don't worry about that. I got here. I'll get us back."

She crawled up on his horse and then he came up behind her.

A shiver of revulsion went through her at how near he was. She could feel his body pressed up against hers and she feared what would happen to her.

Slowly he rode his horse off the property.

"Your tracks are visible in the snow. They'll find you," she said. "It would be better if you let me go. Mack will kill you if he finds you've taken me."

Sitting on the horse, she gripped the pommel on the saddle, trying hard not to touch him.

"Dearest, Beth, I came all this way to claim you. Besides, you owe me. You left me for dead. Six stitches later, a severe headache, and being weak as a kitten for a week, I want revenge."

He thought she was Beth. And she knew what he intended. A shiver of fear rippled along her spine.

She should have contacted the sheriff. He had not been dead.

"Harrison, I'm a decent woman and you were trying to rape me."

"You're a whore just like all women. I would have married you and cleaned out your bank account. All you had to do was say yes, and you refused me."

Beth had never told her that he asked her to marry him.

"You never asked me to marry you."

"True, but when you told me to leave, I knew I didn't love you and never would."

"All you wanted was my inheritance."

The man laughed. "You're a lonely woman. Of course, I could get away with it."

Oh no, he couldn't because Cora watched the accounts very closely.

"How did that work out for you?"

He slapped her on the arm and she knew if he could have gotten to her face, he would have hit her there.

"Beth, once I get you to sign over the accounts to me, it's going to work just fine. Dad kept telling me just to marry one of you and then the money would be ours, but I didn't want to marry either of you."

How would Harrison react when he learned she had closed the accounts in Charleston? That the money was hidden in their clothes. But she wasn't going to tell him for fear of how he would react.

Hopefully by now, those at the cabin realized something had happened and were on their way to find her.

"Again, we will perish if you try to take me back to Charleston. Any day now Mack says we're going to have a blizzard. Can you survive below zero temperatures?"

The thought of that journey was enough to make her fight. He seemed not at all concerned, and she realized, he planned on killing her. There would be no trip back to Charleston. She'd be dead.

"Don't worry, dear. There is a little cabin not too far from here. Lucky for you, I brought the change of account papers with me. All you have to do is sign them and then I'll let you go."

No, he wouldn't. Because then she could contest him and she felt certain he would kill her once she signed those papers. Mack could even now be searching for her.

"So I don't have to return to Charleston with you?"

"Oh no. All you have to do is sign over your bank accounts to me. Then you're free to go."

It sounded way too good to be true and she knew he would not keep his promise. He would shoot her dead and leave her. And he could probably get away with killing her. In Charleston, the law didn't seem to apply to men like him. Would it be the same here?

"All right, I'll sign them," she said, knowing it would be useless because she'd already closed the accounts. "You can have what's in the bank."

"That a girl," he said. "I knew you would come around to my thinking."

# CHAPTER 20

*E*veryone was seated at the breakfast table except Cora. Mack frowned. He heard her go outside to collect the eggs this morning. Had she not returned?

"Where's Cora?"

"She went out to gather the eggs," Hattie said. "That's the last time I saw her."

"That's been at least thirty minutes ago. She should have returned by now," Mack said rising from the table.

He grabbed his hat and coat as he walked out onto the front porch. "Cora?"

It was silent.

Putting on his hat, he slipped on his coat and walked down the steps. James appeared by his side.

"This is not like her," he said.

They walked to the chicken pen and as Mack went to

open the door, James grabbed his arm. "Look. Two sets of footprints in the snow."

They began to follow the footsteps and soon came upon the basket of broken eggs.

Mack cursed. "He's taken her. Here are footprints to horse tracks."

"Let's go," James said. "We're going to kill this son of a bitch."

The women had come out and were standing on the porch. "What's wrong."

"She's been taken," James cried out as he ran to the barn to get the horses.

Hattie ran back inside the house and came out with two rifles and two pistols.

"Here are your guns," she said. "Go get Cora."

Beth started to cry. "It's Harrison. She said she saw him, but I wasn't quite sure I believed her. He's taken her. He'll kill her."

"No," Mack said. "I'm not going to let him harm her. You and Hattie stay here. I'm going to tell the ranch hands to stand guard. This ends today."

While James saddled the horses, he alerted the ranch hands to be prepared and watch to make certain Harrison didn't return. Plus, he sent one man to town for the sheriff. If he didn't have to, he wouldn't kill the man, but would have the law take him into town.

This time the congressman's son would not get away.

When he brought the horses out, Mack had everything ready to go.

"You know there is that old shack a few miles away. He's headed in that direction."

"Let's follow the tracks and see where they lead us," Mack said, trying to remain calm, while inside his emotions wanted revenge.

They rode slowly keeping an eye on where the man was headed.

"You know he's going to set a trap," James said. "Or at least I would. After all, you know your tracks are clearly in the snow. He's got to be prepared."

"True," Mack said. "What would you do?"

"I'd have a trigger set up, that when sprung, slings a knife."

"Man, you're devious. I need to remember that," Mack said, thinking it was a good plan and one he didn't want to encounter. All he wanted to do was reach Cora and rescue her. And this time, she was going to marry him.

"How far from the cabin are we?"

"About half a mile," James said after they had ridden for an hour.

Mack's chest ached. After finding love again, it would be so unfair to lose her like this. It would be so wrong when he hadn't told her he loved her. When he hadn't tried yet again to get her to marry him.

"You know I asked her to marry me and she turned me down," he said, his heart heavy.

James's head jerked toward him. "Did you tell her you loved her?"

"No. At the time the words wouldn't come."

"Have I taught you nothing? You don't ask a woman to marry you without telling her how much you love her. You tell her you can't live without her and how you want her to be the mother of your children. Why in the world is she going to accept your proposal if there is no love involved? You do love her, don't you?"

Mack closed his eyes for just a moment. "Yes, with all my heart and soul. And now I'm terrified I've waited too long to tell her."

James shook his head. "You are the most stubborn man I've ever known. Even worse than our father, who at least, God love him, told our mother on a regular basis how much he loved her. And don't give me any excuses about your first wife. She's dead. She's in the past and it's time to get on."

"You're right," Mack said.

Astonished, James shook his head. "Damn, what a day. My brother tells me he's in love *and* I'm right." He glanced up at the sky. "Lord, protect us because we're going to need it. Mack has had an epiphany. A good one, and I thank you for helping him to see the light. Now get us through this."

Mack glanced at his brother and smiled. "It's good to know you're a praying man."

"Always have been," he said. "That's why Beth and I are getting married Christmas Eve with or without you and Cora."

"Well, let's see about making it a double wedding," Mack said.

Suddenly they saw the shabby cabin nestled in the woods. They heard shouting and it was all Mack could do not to ride his horse into that cabin and shoot Harrison.

"Sign the damn paper," a male voice said. "I've waited long enough for your money."

"Where's your inkwell and pen?" Cora responded. "Or do you want me to sign it in blood?"

"Either way is fine with me. Just sign it, so I can sample what your sister stopped me from doing that night."

James made a motion that he was going to ride around the back. He slid off his horse and Mack followed. "Watch out for trip wires."

Mack nodded.

After James crept around to the back of the cabin, Mack began to search for a trap. Sure enough, there was one. Looking up in the tree, he saw a machete strung tightly between the branches. When his horse hit the wire, the knife would have swung down and hit him in the chest.

Taking out his blade, he cut the wire and the machete fell into the snow. Not one for subtlety. He threw the knife at the front door. It struck the wood. Then he hid in some bushes.

The door yanked open and Harrison glanced around the area as he pulled the knife from the door.

"They're here," he said, pulling out his gun. He stepped back inside and when he returned to the door, he had Cora with the gun pointed at her head.

"If you come any closer, I'm going to shoot her," he yelled.

Mack didn't say a word, but rather let him continue gazing. Then the silly man began to fire his gun at different bushes. Thank goodness, Mack had tied his horse away from the cabin. His bullet hit the dirt next to Mack's boot.

Enough.

With his six-shooters cocked, he stood and approached the man, his guns trained on Harrison. "The sheriff is on his way. I suggest you release her and leave before he arrives."

The man smiled. "No, I'm not through having my fun with Beth."

"That's not Beth, that's Cora," Mack said.

The man stared at Cora. "No, you're wrong. Cora is a vile mean bitch. Besides she's wearing blue and Beth always wears blue."

Cora only stared at the man. She didn't say a word.

"That's really bad when you can't even tell the women apart. Why do you want Beth?"

The man smiled. "I don't want her. I want her money. And now I have the signed bank documents, her money is mine."

He yanked on Cora's arm. "You're interrupting us. We were just about to celebrate her giving me her fortune. After I sample her wares, she'll be saying her good-byes, so ride on cowboy. This is none of your business."

Rage filled Mack at the way the man thought he could get away with hurting Cora.

"Touch her and you're a dead man," Mack said beneath his breath. "She's mine."

The man held his gun up to Cora's forehead and pulled back the trigger.

"Get on down the road, if you don't want me to kill her right now," he said. "The sheriff may arrest me, but my papa is a congressman. I can do whatever I want. So I'd suggest you ride on back to your property and leave us alone. We're conducting some serious banking business and then I'm going to spread her legs and finish what I started that night so many months ago."

Mack took a deep breath. "Last chance. Let her go."

"No. I told you I'll kill her if you shoot me."

"What about me?" James said as he poked his gun into the man's back and then proceeded to knock the gun from Harrison's hand. "I'm just itching to shoot you. So please go ahead and try something. Beth, my fiancée, is at home where she belongs. She told me what you tried to do to her and I'd like nothing more than to let a stray bullet put an end to your rakish behavior."

A smile crossed Mack's face. One thing he loved about his brother was his way with words.

Harrison dropped his hold on Cora and she kicked him in the shin. "I'm Cora, and by the way, that bank paperwork is useless. Those accounts have been closed. There is no money in Charleston."

Dumbfounded, he glanced at her as he rubbed his leg. "You bitch. You tricked me."

"No, I outsmarted you," she said and ran to Mack.

He pulled her into his arms and kissed her on the lips. "Thank God. You scared the hell out of me woman."

"I knew you would come," she said, sinking into his embrace.

"Let me help James tie him up and then we're going home. We've got a lot to talk about."

Mack took a chair outside of the cabin and pushed Harrison down and then they tied his ankles and his wrists to the arms and legs. He was immobile.

James clenched his fists. "I'd like to take a swing at you, but it's not fair to a defenseless coward like yourself. You tried to hurt my Beth and that's not acceptable. Come near her again and you're a dead man."

He turned to Mack and frowned.

"Take Cora home. I'll sit with our friend here until the sheriff arrives," James said.

Mack wasn't certain he liked that idea, but then again, maybe it was for the best.

"Don't kill him. Let the law do the work. He thinks his papa is going to save him, but he doesn't realize he's in the Montana territory. Our laws are not the same as the states."

Harrison's face turned white. "Montana is not a state?"

"Not yet," James said. "Your papa cannot help you here."

The man cursed, and for the first time, Mack could see genuine fear on his face.

"Mack, take me home before I'm tempted to find another fireplace poker and make certain this time he really is dead," she said.

A grin swept over Mack's face as he scooped Cora up and carried her to his horse. Then he crawled up behind her. Leaning down, his lips covered hers in a kiss that told her what his heart was feeling, but his brain withheld.

Not any longer.

He released her lips and stared down at her. He couldn't wait another moment. Already they had wasted so much time, and while this might not be as romantic as most proposals, he didn't care.

"Darling, I thought I'd lost you. I've already lost one love and I can't lose a second one. You've captured my heart, my soul, and made me into a happy man. No longer am I considered grumpy Mack. I love you more than the moon and the stars and heaven above. Please marry me and be the mother of my children, my wife, and my lover. For without your love, I'm going to be the grumpiest man in Montana."

Her brown eyes filled with tears. "We can't have you being the grumpiest man in Montana. All I was waiting to hear was that you loved me. You're the first and only person to tell me you love me and I can't live without you. Yes, I will be the mother of your children, your wife, and your lover."

She reached up and stroked the side of his face. "Forever and ever, until I take my last breath."

Mack grabbed the sides of her mouth, his lips covering hers and claiming her. This was all he ever wanted. An everlasting love. And this time, he was certain he'd gotten it right.

# CHAPTER 21

$\mathcal{C}$hristmas Eve, the church was filled to capacity with the residents of Angel Creek.

Cora glanced out the door at the people filling the pews. So many she didn't know, but she didn't care. Tonight in a double-ring ceremony, Beth and she were marrying their heroes.

Hattie had surprised them by making them each a bridal veil. She didn't have enough material for a white wedding gown. All but two ranch hands had come to town with them and tonight they would be staying at the Rose Haven boarding house.

"We're getting married, Cora," Beth said almost breathlessly. "And it's all because of you. If you had not almost killed Harrison, we would not have answered that ad that brought us to Angel Creek. We're getting married on the holiest day of the year."

Tears filled Cora's eyes. "Good ole Harrison. I hear

he found out that his father being a congressman in North Carolina didn't mean much. Especially when Montana is not part of the United States."

Beth giggled. "I can't believe he thought that he had kidnapped *me*. What does that tell you? He didn't even know me well enough to recognize the differences between us. James has never confused us. Never."

"No, he hasn't," Cora said, trying to get a glimpse of Mack. Tonight he would make her his wife and she couldn't be any happier. She loved him more than she could ever believe and couldn't imagine life without him.

"The church is so beautiful. It's decorated with such gorgeous colors. And our men are waiting for us at the front."

Just then, the congregation seemed to quiet down and everyone took their seats.

"Oh my, we're about to get married," Beth said. "It's happening."

Cora reached over and gave her sister a hug. "I don't think I've ever told you this before, but I love you. I'm making it my vow that from this day forward, I'm telling the people I care about how much I love them. Mack was first and now you, Beth."

Tears rolled down Beth's cheeks. "I love you too, Cora. Our parents never said that to us, and on the day Jesus was born, we're going to start doing better. I like your idea. James knows I love him, but we need to remember to tell our children as well."

A smile crossed Cora's face. "I agree. Now let's go marry those two gorgeous men of ours."

They shut the door right before the preacher's wife knocked. Beth opened the door to Ginger Carroll, who was at least six months pregnant. "Ladies, it's time to marry your men. Merry Christmas!"

# CHAPTER 22

*1*928 Christmas Eve

It was the fiftieth anniversary of the church in Angel Creek. The little town had grown and the original families were now elderly.

Cora gazed out at the people she had known for years.

Charity and Lewis Brown were here with their children, grandchildren, and great-grandchildren. There was a whole brood of people from their family. Lewis had sold the saloon years ago, and together, he and Charity were living with their oldest daughter and her family. During Christmas, Charity still made certain that everyone received a small gift during the holidays. It was her donation to the community.

Flint and Ginger Carroll had been with the church for many years until Flint retired at the age of eighty to spend more time with his grandsons. But he still worked around the church and helped the new preacher. Their family was here with three sons and two daughters and all their children and grandchildren.

Ginger's hair was gray, but she always wore a smile and would look to Flint to make certain he was all right. Last year, he'd suddenly fallen unconscious and woke unable to move one side of his body. And now, she watched over him and encouraged him to rest.

They knew they were in their last years, but their love was so strong between them, they didn't want to leave the other behind.

Tripp and Minnie Maddox were here with their six children and their grandchildren. Tripp was looking older and wasn't moving quite as quickly as he did before, but he stood proudly beside his wife, always at her side, protecting her. Their love story was one that even Cora couldn't believe.

But the love she saw in the couple's eyes was rock solid. And their family was the center of their universe. Their daughter Beth had become a doctor and she and her physician husband had set up a practice here in Angel Creek. Born on Christmas Eve in a barn, she was a beautiful story that brought her parents together. A story that even Cora had told her own children.

Flint walked to the church podium and smiled out at the people in attendance.

"Thank you for coming to celebrate the anniversary of the church and the Christmas Eve service. The last fifty years have sped by and so many of the founding families now have great-great-grandchildren. We have so much to be thankful for. God has blessed all of us. I'd like to mention Anna Jackson who died back in 1915 and Levi, her husband who passed two years later. Their family is here to help celebrate the church they belonged to."

For a moment, Flint teared up. "I'd also like to thank my lovely wife, Ginger, who has been the foundation of my life. Who I could not do without. My love for you has no end."

People clapped.

"She made me into a much better preacher and filled our home with so much love. Thank you."

Ginger blew him a kiss, their children and grandchildren surrounding her.

"Now, I'd like to turn it over to the new preacher. He will lead us forward into the next fifty years. While many of us will be resting in heaven, he will guide the church into the future where I hear there are now automobiles instead of horses."

The congregation laughed.

"Pastor Charles, may the life of this congregation be richly blessed."

Flint turned and walked away from the podium.

The new preacher stood before the congregation.

"Look around you, folks. These are the people who made our small town into the best place on earth. These are the pioneers who braved the blizzards, the hardships, and the tragedies and came out on top. Because of these people, Angel Creek is a wonderful place to live."

The congregation clapped.

"From the mail order brides who arrived from Charleston, to the men who took a chance on love and now are surrounded by their families. God is good and we have so much to be thankful for on this Christmas Eve. Join with me as we begin the celebration of Christ's birth."

The entire church stood and Cora looked down the row at her own family. Mack was holding their latest great-grandson, who at the age of two, liked to get into trouble. With five boys and three girls, their children were all married and they now had ten great-grand-children.

She couldn't help but think back to the first Christmas when they were married in this very church.

Mack turned to look at her and smiled, knowing she was remembering their first Christmas together. Every day, he still left her a message, telling her how much he loved her. Today, his message said,

*Dearest Cora,*

*You're the best thing that has ever happened to me. I'm so thankful to Harrison Dane for bringing us together. This old heart will always be yours.*

*Love,*

*Mack*

Every day, she thanked God she had taken a chance and married him.

She watched as he pulled out the watch she'd given him that first Christmas and read the inscription: *Time started with you.*

And it had. Her life had begun when Mack married her.

Their lives had been filled with good times and bad. The death of Hattie, then her sister Beth. And eventually James. Two more babies were buried beside his first son, and instead of tearing them apart, they had grieved and mourned each death together.

Whatever storm life gave them, they faced it together.

Every morning, they said *I love you* and every night before they went to bed, they kissed goodnight and again mentioned their love for one another.

The days of their lives were growing shorter and she couldn't imagine not having Mack by her side.

But regardless of how much time they had left together, he had given her a wonderful life filled with the family she had always dreamed of. While they didn't have a perfect life, they had a perfect love and she had so much to be thankful for.

With tears in her eyes, she said thank you to God who had led a young, scared woman, who thought she had killed a man, to this beautiful town and this man who showed her the true meaning of love.

Opening her eyes, she knew this was going to be the best Christmas ever as she joined the congregation in singing.

* * *

Sadly this is the last book in this series. After twenty-three books, the authors decided it was time to end Angel Creek Christmas Brides. We hope you have enjoyed these Christmas stories as much as we've enjoyed writing them. Mack and Cora's story was the perfect ending for this author. Two people who did not want to marry, who fell in love.

If you're inclined, please leave a review. Reviews help authors.

# PLEASE LEAVE A REVIEW

Did you enjoy the book? Reviews help authors. I would appreciate you posting a review.

Follow Sylvia McDaniel on Facebook.
Join my Readers Group on Facebook!

**Sign up for my New Book Alert and receive a free book.**

Charleston isn't what it used to be. The war has left it in ruins and the chance of a suitable marriage almost obsolete. Five friends take a daring leap and head west for a new life and possible love match as Mail-Order brides. After finding their happily ever afters, they invite more of their friends to join them, and soon, Angel Creek, Montana is invaded by Southern Belles all looking for love and the town will never be the same.

**CHRISTMAS 2018 BOOKS**
Book 1: **Charity** — Sylvia McDaniel
Book 2: **Julia** — Lily Graison
Book 3: **Ruby** — Hildie McQueen
Book 4: **Sarah** — Peggy McKenzie
Book 5: **Anna** — Everly West

**CHRISTMAS 2019 BOOKS**
Book 6: **Caroline** — Lily Graison
Book 7: **Melody** — Caroline Clemmons
Book 8: **Emma** — Peggy McKenzie
Book 9: **Viola** — Cyndi Raye
Book 10: **Ginger** — Sylvia McDaniel

**CHRISTMAS 2020 BOOKS**

**Book 11: Abigail** — Peggy McKenzie
**Book 12: Pearl** — Hildie McQueen
**Book 13: Rebecca** — Lily Graison
**Book 14: Charlotte** — Kari Trumbo
**Book 15: Minnie** — Sylvia McDaniel
**Book 16: Adele** — Cynthia Woolf
**Book 17: Victoria** — Maxine Douglas
**Book 18: Meg** — Caroline Clemmons

**CHRISTMAS 2021 BOOKS**
**Book 19: Glenda** — Hildie McQueen
**Book 20: Temperance** — Lily Graison
**Book 21: Hannah** — Peggy McKenzie
**Book 22: Amy** — Caroline Clemmons
**Book 23: Cora** — Sylvia McDaniel

## Western Historicals
A Hero's Heart
Second Chance Cowboy
Ethan

## American Brides
**Katie: Bride of Virginia

## Angel Creek Christmas Brides
**Charity
**Ginger
**Minne
**Cora
Angel Creek Christmas Box Set

## Bad Girls of the West
Scandalous Sadie
Ravenous Rose
Tempting Tessa
Nellie's Redemption
Bad Girls Box Set

## The Burnett Brides Series
The Rancher Takes A Bride
The Outlaw Takes A Bride
The Marshal Takes A Bride
The Christmas Bride
Boxed Set

## Lipstick and Lead Series
Desperate

Deadly

Dangerous

Daring

Determined

Deceived

Defiant

Devious

Lipstick and Lead Box Set Books 1-4

Lipstick and Lead Box Set Books 5-9

Lipstick and Lead Box Set Books 1-9

**Quinlan's Quest

## Mail Order Bride Tales
**A Brother's Betrayal

**Pearl

**Ace's Bride

## Scandalous Suffragettes of the West
**Abigail

Bella

Mistletoe Scandal

## Southern Historical Romance
A Scarlet Bride

## The Cuvier Women
Wronged

Betrayed
Beguiled
Boxed Set

**The Debutante's of Durango**
The Debutante's Scandal
The Debutante's Gamble
The Debutante's Revenge
The Debutante's Santa
Box Set

**\*\* Denotes a sweet book.**

**Want to learn about my new releases before anyone else? Sign up for my New Book Alert and receive a complimentary book.**

USA Today Best-selling author Sylvia McDaniel obviously has too much time on her hands. With over one hundred Western historical and contemporary romance novels, she spends most days torturing her characters. Bad boys deserve punishment, and even good girls get into trouble. Always looking for the next plot twist, she's known for her sweet, funny, family-oriented romances.

Married to her best friend for over twenty-five years, they recently moved to the state of Colorado, where they like to hike and enjoy the beauty of the forest behind their home with their spoiled dachshund Zeus. (He has his own column in her newsletter.)

Their grown son still lives in Texas. An avid football watcher, she loves the Broncos and the Cowboys, especially when they're winning.

www.SylviaMcDaniel.com
The End